"Good job. Looks like the tube is in place." His low voice was reassuring. Almost mesmerizing. Relief made Hannah's knees feel weak, but she stiffened them with an effort. Her job was only partially done. "You'll need to get a chest X-ray to confirm placement."

"Will do," she said, as she handed over the task of securing the tube to the nurse standing beside her. Once she was free to move aside, she glanced up at her rescuer.

And froze when his glittering green gaze slammed into hers.

The force of the collision made her heart drop to the soles of her feet. The room whirled and there was a loud roaring in her ears.

No. It couldn't be. But it was.

Jake. Her Jake. Her one-night-stand-Jake was here.

The flare of shock reflected in his gaze almost made her feel better. At least she wasn't the only one knocked off-balance at seeing him again. But then she noticed the name on his ID badge and the sick feeling in her gut returned.

Great. Just what she needed. Not only was Jake a doctor here at the hospital.

He was Dr. Holt. The attending physician on duty. And the Chief of Trauma Surgery!

The man she'd impulsively spent the night with was the same man who could make or break her career.

Dear Reader

When I was young, I wanted to be a doctor. (Didn't we all?) However, back then women didn't have quite the same opportunities as men, and following that career path required a huge time commitment. So I settled on becoming a nurse instead.

I've always admired those who did make the sacrifice needed to become a doctor. So I decided to write a story where the heroine becomes a surgeon against the most overwhelming odds.

Hannah Stewart has studied hard and worked several jobs on her path to becoming a surgeon. She's determined that nothing and no one will get in her way. Including the hot Chief of Trauma Surgery Jake Holt. After an incredible night with Hannah, Jake is stunned to discover she is one of his new interns, assigned to the trauma rotation. A relationship between them is completely out of the question. Or is it?

I hope you enjoy Hannah and Jake's story. Don't hesitate to visit my website or find me on Facebook. I love to hear from my readers.

Sincerely

Laura Iding

www.lauraiding.com

DATING
DR DELICIOUS

BY
LAURA IDING

First published in Great Britain 2011
by Mills & Boon, an imprint of Harlequin (UK) Limited,
Eton House, 18-24 Paradise Road, Richmond, Surrey TW9 1SR

© Laura Iding 2011

ISBN: 978 0 263 22072 8

Harlequin (UK) policy is to use papers that are natural, renewable and recyclable products and made from wood grown in sustainable forests. The logging and manufacturing process conform to the legal environmental regulations of the country of origin.

Printed and bound in Great Britain
by CPI Antony Rowe, Chippenham, Wiltshire

Laura Iding loved reading as a child, and when she ran out of books she readily made up her own, completing a little detective mini-series when she was twelve. But, despite her aspirations for being an author, her parents insisted she look into a 'real' career. So the summer after she turned thirteen she volunteered as a Candy Striper, and fell in love with nursing. Now, after twenty years of experience in trauma/critical care, she's thrilled to combine her career and her hobby into one—writing Medical™ Romances for Mills & Boon. Laura lives in the northern part of the United States, and spends all her spare time with her two teenage kids (help!)—a daughter and a son—and her husband. Enjoy!

Recent titles by the same author:

A KNIGHT FOR NURSE HART
THE NURSE'S BROODING BOSS
THE SURGEON'S NEW-YEAR WEDDING WISH
EXPECTING A CHRISTMAS MIRACLE

CHAPTER ONE

HANNAH Stewart woke up, momentarily confused by the darkness. Then she remembered.

There were no lights from the city shining in through her curtainless windows because she wasn't at home. She was at Jake's condo.

An odd mixture of pleasure and shame washed over her. Good heavens, what in the world had gotten into her? Allowing Jake to take her to his place last night had been completely out of character. Yet she couldn't bring herself to regret her impulsive decision.

Or rather she refused to regret one second of the pleasure she'd spent in Jake's arms.

But fantasy time was over. Carefully, she lifted her head from the pillow to better read the small alarm clock on the bedside table. It was half past three in the morning.

Late. Or early. Depending on your frame of reference.

Regardless, she needed to leave. Now. Her last day of freedom was over and she needed to get home and pull herself together before heading to the hospital.

Gently, so as not to wake the man sleeping soundly beside her, she eased out from beneath the covers. When she stood, taking her weight off the mattress, Jake muttered and shifted restlessly. She froze, holding her breath until she was reassured he hadn't woken up.

Daring to breathe again, she blindly felt around the floor for her clothes, before remembering that she'd likely left most of them in the living room.

The memory of their frantic lovemaking made her blush. Never before had she let herself go so freely as the way she had with the devilishly attractive Jake. She'd lost count of how many times they'd made love. Her body still ached in the most unusual places.

She slipped from the bedroom and headed down the hall, into the living room. She stubbed her toe on the glass-and-chrome coffee table and had to bite her tongue to keep from crying out in pain. In the flurry of sexual activity, she'd only gotten a glimpse of the interior of Jake's condo, but as her eyes adjusted to the dim light from the window, she looked around curiously.

She wrinkled her nose, somewhat disappointed to see that he went for the expensive, modern type of dcor. Not that it mattered, except the chrome and glass seemed a bit impersonal. And the so-called art on the walls made her raise her eyebrows in surprise.

Hmm. She obviously didn't get it.

The sense of shame intensified. She didn't belong in the world of sailboats, yachts and fancy high-rise condos. And she'd been silly even to try. Once she became a surgeon, she still couldn't imagine herself living like this. She'd gone into medicine to help people, not to become rich and famous.

Fantasy time was definitely over.

Shaking her head at her foolishness, she picked up

her clothes, strewn from one corner of the room to the other. She blushed again as she pulled on her yellow bikini, limping as she favored her sore toe. She pulled on the blouse and shorts over the top, slipped her feet into her flip-flop sandals and reached for her purse.

"Going somewhere?" Jake asked.

Her heart shot into her throat and she gasped, spinning around toward him. He stood in the hallway wearing nothing but a scowl on his face and low-slung boxers. Refusing to be distracted by his muscular bare chest, she tried to keep her gaze steady as the seconds dragged out into a long, uncomfortable minute. "Yes. I—uh, have to go."

His gaze bored into hers. "Without saying goodbye?"

Embarrassed, she glanced away. Okay, maybe she was out of practice with this stuff but, really, what did he expect? They didn't even know each other's last names.

She shoved aside the flash of guilt. People did this all the time, right? Right. "Look, it was great. Spectacular, really. You were…absolutely amazing. But I have an important meeting to attend this morning so I really need to get home."

His gaze never wavered. "Fine. I'll drive you."

"No!" Her refusal came out more harshly than she'd intended. But for some reason she wasn't anxious for him to know where she lived. Besides, from this day forward her life was not her own. She had no idea what he did for work, but whatever it was, she was certain he'd have far more free time than she would. "I mean, don't bother. I'll get a cab." Or the subway.

"Hannah," he protested, starting toward her, but she picked up her purse and quickly opened the door, effectively cutting him off.

"Goodbye, Jake. You'll never know how badly I needed what we shared last night. Thanks for everything." She slipped out of the condo and hastily walked down the hall to the elevators. She held her breath, hoping, praying he didn't follow.

When the elevator dinged, she couldn't help throwing a glance over her shoulder, surprised to discover he'd followed her out. Standing there, his broad-muscled shoulder propped up against the wall and his arms crossed over his chest, he looked incredibly sexy, especially with the way his tousled black hair framed his hard, chiseled face.

A wave of regret hit hard and she stumbled, almost falling flat on her face.

Dear God, he was like a giant magnet pulling every cell in her body back toward him. She really, really didn't want to leave.

But she had to.

It took every ounce of willpower she possessed to regain her equilibrium, flashing him a weak smile and a tiny wave before disappearing inside the waiting elevator.

As the doors closed she heard him murmur, "Goodbye, Hannah."

She closed her eyes and slumped against the wall of the elevator, running a hand through her hopelessly tangled hair. Tears of regret stung her eyes and she quickly swiped them away. What in the world was wrong with her?

He was just a man. An incredibly sexy, fiercely attractive man, yes. But still a man.

It was better to make a clean break. As much as she had enjoyed being with him, she didn't have time for a man.

Or a relationship.

Not that Jake had even remotely offered such a thing, she reminded herself sternly.

People had one-night stands all the time, and she was pretty sure none of the participants stood around dissecting every moment after the fact. So why was she second-guessing herself? Sex was good. Sex was healthy. They'd had a great time together and now it was over.

End of discussion.

Hannah hailed a cab and rode through the dark streets to the less glitzy part of town. The warehouse apartment she shared with Margie was scantily and eclectically furnished, but boasted huge windows along two walls. True to form, her roommate wasn't home. Margie had obviously spent the night with her boyfriend, Bryan.

Relieved to discover that Margie wasn't there to grill her over what had happened, she made her way to her bedroom.

Normally she liked to drink a cup of coffee while looking out at the sun rising over the water, but today she was too anxious to try to relax so she simply showered and dressed. The subway ride to the hospital didn't take long and she made it to Chicago Care with fifteen minutes to spare.

Thank God she wasn't late on her very first day. In fact, she felt oddly energized.

A night of spectacular sex could do that for you.

She tried her best to wipe the crooked grin off her face.

The general-surgery conference room on the fifth floor contained about thirty-five people—interns, just like herself, waiting to start their first day as doctors.

A sliver of anticipation mixed with a healthy dose of fear filled her chest. This was it. The moment she'd been waiting for. She was officially a doctor.

Dr. Hannah Stewart.

Yesterday, she'd celebrated the end of her old life. The eight-year grind of working, studying and then working some more. Balancing two jobs to support herself and her family while managing to keep decent grades through medical school hadn't been easy. She'd spent most of her time during medical school alone. Hadn't she deserved one night of fun, of recklessness? Of letting loose and having fun? Of doing something just for herself and no one else?

Maybe she'd taken her celebration a little too far by going home to spend the night with Jake, but that didn't matter. There was no point in ruminating over the past. She was moving on to the next stage of her career. She'd waited for this day for what seemed like forever. Growing up, they'd lived from one paycheck to the next. And, truthfully, her years of college and medical school hadn't been much different. Even with a massive loan to pay her tuition, she'd still struggled to make ends meet.

Despite the odds that had been steeply stacked against her from the moment she'd left high school, she'd made it. She'd passed her medical boards. She'd been accepted into the surgical residency program.

Hannah lifted her chin stubbornly. She'd made it

this far, and she was bound and determined to make it through the grueling five years before her, too.

Nothing and no one was going to stand in her way.

Hannah was sharply disappointed to discover the entire first two days of being a new intern meant being stuck in new-employee orientation training for hours on end. Granted, the information was obviously important, and full of rules she tried hard to commit to memory, but sitting in the large lecture hall had been extremely anticlimactic.

Being with her fellow interns wasn't too bad. She bonded a little bit with one of the few female residents, a strikingly beautiful caramel-skinned young woman by the name of Andrea Barkley. It was a little disturbing to know that the odds were, in fact, stacked against them. The surgical residency program was brutal, one of the reasons many women rarely got in. Or, if they did get in, they didn't make it all the way through the program.

Or so she'd heard from her former boyfriend, Alec, who had been an intern when she'd been a junior medical student. No wonder their brief relationship hadn't lasted very long.

The jerk hadn't been the least bit supportive of her dream to become a surgeon. In fact, she'd had the sense he was threatened by her knowledge and determination. As if they were in some sort of competition or something. He never hesitated to make her feel stupid. And he wasn't supportive of her family issues, either. Or of her need to work two jobs.

She was much better off without him.

For a moment the image of Jake's laughing face filled her mind. She ruthlessly shoved it aside.

She didn't have time for men. Even one as sexy and charming as Jake. There was no point in wondering if Jake would be supportive of her chosen career. Or supportive of her messed-up family.

Jake would be nothing more than a distraction she couldn't afford.

Hannah met up with Andrea in the female surgical-residency locker room on the third day, relieved to discover they had been assigned to the same rotation, trauma surgery, for the month of July. Today was their first day taking care of real, live patients.

Hannah proudly donned her knee-length lab coat over her scrubs. The medical students were forced to wear short lab coats so that it was clear to the hospital staff that they were only students.

Now it would be clear to the hospital staff that she was a doctor. A surgical resident responsible for treating patients. She tucked her stethoscope into her pocket and took a deep breath.

She could do this. She'd studied hard and trained for this.

"Are you nervous?" Hannah whispered to Andrea as they walked down to the busy arena, the heart of activity in any emergency department. There were patients everywhere. Patients that were counting on them as residents to have a clue as to what might be wrong with them.

She quickly squelched the sliver of self-doubt.

"No." Andrea glanced at her for a long moment and then shrugged. "Okay, maybe a little."

"Yeah. Me, too."

They walked up and introduced themselves to the senior resident on Trauma, Dr. Richard Reynolds.

He didn't look thrilled to be saddled with two new residents. Did he have a grudge against females being in the program? Hannah wasn't sure, but remained determined to prove him wrong, no matter what his assumptions were.

"There are a couple of trauma patients on the way in from a motor-vehicle crash," Richard said. "I want each of you to take one of the patients. The attending on call today is Dr. Holt and both of us will be here if you need help. Any questions?"

Traumas? On their first day caring for patients? The look on the senior resident's face was almost sneering, as if he expected them to balk at the responsibility. So Hannah straightened her shoulders and lifted her chin. "No questions."

His gaze narrowed a bit, but then he nodded. "Good."

Just then the doors from the ambulance bay burst open and two gurneys were wheeled in. For a moment panic stole her breath, but then a sense of calm came over her, as she took control of the first patient.

"James Turkow is a twenty-five-year-old restrained driver T-boned by another vehicle," the paramedic announced. "Vitals were stable, and he was alert and oriented on the scene, but during transport became less responsive."

Probable head injury, Hannah decided. But the bluish tint to his lips was concerning, so she pulled her stethoscope from her pocket and quickly listened to his lungs. Definitely not good. From what she could tell, he wasn't moving nearly enough air to sustain life.

"Get me the intubation tray," she ordered, pulling the oxygen mask and ambu-bag off the regulator on the wall to begin bagging him. With a flick of her wrist she turned the oxygen up to one hundred percent. "This guy needs an airway."

The nurse quickly pulled out the emergency airway kit, handing over a laryngoscope and blade. "What size tube?"

"Eight." Hannah quickly pulled on gloves and then took a deep breath to calm her racing heart. While the nurse placed the stylet into the endotracheal tube, she gently inserted the blade into her patient's mouth and pulled upward—the way she had been taught—to search for his vocal cords.

Except she didn't see them.

For a moment panic surged, and she frantically glanced around for Richard, the senior resident. Where in the heck was he? Didn't he know she might need help? But Richard wasn't readily available, so she tried again, tipping the young man's head back farther and looking once again, down the back of his throat. Her left hand wielded the laryngoscope and she pulled upward, keeping away from his teeth to avoid damaging them.

"Easy, now, you're doing fine," a deep male voice said near her ear. Just knowing she wasn't alone was enough to calm her frayed nerves. "Pull up just a little more. There, see the cords?"

Amazingly, she did see them. Trying to hold her left hand steady, she used her right hand to thread the ETT down through the patient's vocal cords.

"Excellent," the voice murmured. "Now remove the stylet and begin bagging. I'll take a listen to make sure you're in the right spot."

She nodded, taking care to keep the tube firmly in place as she did as he requested. She kept her gaze trained on the patient's chest, noticing with satisfaction that the chest rose and fell with every breath she gave with the ambu-bag.

"Good job. Looks like the tube is in place." His low voice was reassuring. Almost mesmerizing. Relief made her knees feel weak, but she stiffened them with an effort. Her job was only partially done. "You'll need to get a chest X-ray to confirm placement."

"Will do," she said, as she handed over the task of securing the tube to the nurse standing beside her. Once she was free to move aside, she glanced up at her rescuer.

And froze, when his glittering green gaze slammed into hers.

The force of the collision made her heart plummet, the room whirled and there was a loud roaring in her ears.

No. It couldn't be. But it was.

Jake. Her Jake. Her one-night-stand-Jake was here. At Chicago Care.

The flare of shock reflected in his gaze almost made her feel better. At least she wasn't the only one knocked off balance. But then she noticed the name on his ID badge and the sick feeling in her gut returned.

Great. Just what she needed. Not only was Jake a doctor here at the hospital. He was Dr. Holt. The attending physician on duty. And Chief of Trauma Surgery!

The man she'd impulsively spent the night with was the man who could make or break her career.

CHAPTER TWO

JAKE could hardly believe his eyes when he saw Hannah wearing light blue scrubs and a long white lab coat, her long blonde hair pulled back in some sort of fancy braid. Dr. Stewart. The name on her ID tag mocked him.

Hannah—the girl he'd seen on the sailboat wearing the bright yellow bikini—was an intern? A first-year surgical resident? Here at Chicago Care?

A stab of betrayal hit hard.

She'd known all along exactly who he was.

Hard to believe he was stupid enough to have made the same mistake twice in one lifetime, but he had. Swallowing the lump of bitterness in the back of his throat, he forced himself to keep his attention on the task at hand. There was a seriously injured patient needing their assistance, so this was hardly the time, or the place, to call Hannah out on her behavior.

But she'd certainly played her role well, that's for sure. He'd taken the bait, falling for the ploy without once considering he'd been set up.

Tearing his gaze away from hers, he glanced down at the patient. "Order a stat chest X-ray to verify this tube placement," he said to the nurse. "And I also want a full set of labs."

The nurse headed for the nearest phone.

When he turned back toward Hannah, he noticed she was continuing her trauma assessment as another nurse drew the blood. Clearly, Hannah wasn't nearly as shocked to see him as he was to recognize her.

"His lung sounds are very diminished on the right side," Hannah said, pulling the stethoscope from her ears. "And his belly is tense, no bowel sounds present. He probably has a head injury, seeing as he's still unconscious. So far, though, his pupils are equal and reactive."

Trying very hard not to remember what she'd looked like naked, he gave a curt nod. "Okay, so what's your plan?"

"Get a CT of his head, chest and abdomen, continue to monitor his neuro status closely."

"Fine. Let me know as soon as you have some diagnostic results." He moved away, intending to check on the second patient in the motor-vehicle crash. Richard was assisting the other female intern, Dr. Barkley, with that one, and from what he could tell, they had the patient under control.

Hannah's patient was by far the sicker of the two.

"Dr. Holt?" Hannah's familiar husky voice caused a reaction deep down, making him grind his teeth in frustration. He refused to be made a fool of again.

"What?" he snapped.

"The chest X-ray has been completed, but his abdomen is growing more tense by the minute," she said, pulling aside the hospital gown to show him. "I think he's bleeding internally. Do you want me to perform a peritoneal lavage?"

He didn't want to be impressed by her sharp assessment skills, or the way she managed to remain calm in the middle of a crisis. "Have you done one before?"

"Yes." Even as she responded, Hannah pulled out the peritoneal-lavage tray and began prepping the patient. If she was nervous, she didn't let on. Once the patient's skin was prepped, she pulled on a pair of sterile gloves and then carefully measured two centimeters above the umbilicus. Using the scalpel, she made a quick incision.

"Nice job," he said, before he could stop himself. Once she'd deftly inserted the catheter, she opened up the IV of fluid and then watched, as he did, for the results. He wasn't surprised she'd been right, when bloody drainage came flowing out. "Guess this guy has earned a trip to the O.R."

Hannah's eyes widened a bit. "Right now?"

"As soon as possible. But we need to know the status of his labs before we go anywhere."

"His hemoglobin is low at ten," one of the nurses reported. "And he's not oxygenating very well, either, with a PO two of seventy-eight."

"Transfuse two units of blood now, and then make sure he has four units of blood on hand at all times."

"I bet he's bleeding from a liver laceration," Hannah said.

"Why do you think that? Why not his spleen?" he challenged.

"His spleen could be the source of his bleeding, but he was on the driver's side and wearing his seat belt, which means most of the pressure would have been on the right side, over his liver." Hannah kept her gaze focused on the bloody drainage coming out of the peritoneal catheter as she spoke. "If the injury had been lower, his bowel might be affected, but in that case, we'd likely see intestinal contents mixed in with the blood."

As much as it annoyed him, he agreed with her. "Yes, we would."

"So he might need a liver resection?" Hannah asked.

"Possibly, but that depends on the source of the bleeding. Could be a blood vessel and not the organ itself." He glanced at the nurse. "Where's the chest X-ray?"

"Right here, Dr. Holt."

Jake glanced at the chest X-ray one of the nurses pulled up on the computer monitor at the bedside. He frowned and gestured to it. "And what do you see here?"

"A pneumothorax in the right lower lobe." Hannah finally looked directly at him, her blue gaze seriously intent. "He needs a chest tube before he goes to the O.R."

"Have you done one?"

There was the slightest hesitation. "I've assisted with one," she murmured.

He was tempted to put the damn thing in himself, but this was a teaching institution and he was obligated to at least give her a chance. "I'll talk you through it," he said.

Hannah was already getting the supplies ready. Once the chest-tube insertion tray was open and ready to go, Hannah prepped the right side of their patient's chest and then picked up the scalpel. She made a one-inch incision between the fourth and fifth ribs, but it was too shallow.

"You'll need to go deeper in order to get through the

cartilage," he instructed, coming up behind her, to once again peer over her shoulder as she worked.

He hadn't known who she was when he'd helped her intubate this very same patient, but now it seemed as if every one of his senses were on red alert. Being this close was difficult. The familiar vanilla scent of her skin tormented him.

He watched as she took a deep, bracing breath and then ran the blade through the incision again, going deeper this time. Then she used the tip of her finger to make sure the opening went all the way through. Using the trocar, she inserted the chest tube into the opening.

"Suture it in place," he said, forcing himself to step back. Distance. He needed to keep as much distance as possible. "We don't want that tube coming out on the trip to the O.R."

"Will do." The look of satisfaction on her face almost made him want to smile. Almost. "Will I get a chance to scrub in on this case with you?" she asked.

The softening he'd felt toward her quickly evaporated. This was exactly what she'd wanted, wasn't it? This was why she'd set him up at the marina bar, Shipwrecked, and had flirted with him.

Because she'd wanted to advance her career. He could see the plan she'd formulated in her mind—get intimate with the attending and receive special treatment.

"Not this time, Dr. Stewart," he said bluntly, even though in reality this was the best procedure for an intern to scrub in on. But too bad. He needed an assistant, but he'd get Richard to come into the O.R. with him.

The flash of surprised hurt in her gaze almost

made him change his mind. But she forced a smile. "I understand."

Did she? Because he sure as hell didn't.

Images flashed through his mind, the way he'd taken her frantically up against the wall. And then again, when he'd gently tossed her onto his bed and she'd laughed.

Damn, but she was beautiful. So full of life. A breath of fresh air compared to the other women he'd tried to go out with since the fiasco with Allie. The moment he'd seen Hannah, the instant flare of attraction had stunned him speechless.

Discovering she'd played him for a fool was a cruel twist of fate.

"I'll just observe, then," she continued, as if he wasn't in the middle of an internal war.

"Fine." He turned to find Richard, knee deep in assisting the other intern, Andrea Barkley, with a full-blown trauma resuscitation on their second patient. He scowled. What in the hell had happened? The patient had been stable last time he'd checked. But as he watched for a few minutes, he knew that he couldn't drag Richard away from this case. Not now.

Resigned, he turned back to Hannah. "Actually, I will need your help in the O.R. after all."

"Really? Thank you!" she exclaimed earnestly, her eyes bright with excitement.

For a moment he railed at the unfairness of it all. She looked so enticing. So eager to learn. He tore his gaze away with an effort, and then turned his attention back to his patient. If he could get the internal bleeding under control, this guy would make it.

This should be his priority right now. Saving James

Turkow's young life. Not worrying about Hannah's ulterior motives for sleeping with him.

One month, he thought grimly. He'd be forced to work with her for one month. Surely he could manage to keep his professional distance from her for a measly thirty days.

Hannah was proud at how well she managed to hide her internal emotional turmoil as she assisted Jake in doing the exploratory lap on their blunt-trauma patient.

Concentrating on the surgical technique he employed wasn't easy, especially the way his sexy voice, as he gave instructions, filled her head.

Listening to him speak in a low tone reminded her of their night together. And she had to block her emotional reaction to him as she concentrated on what he was doing.

"See? Here's the grade-four liver laceration," Jake said, gently moving the intestines aside to show her the extent of the injury.

"Looks like the bleeding has stopped," she murmured.

"Yes. For now. We'll have to keep a close eye on this, though, to make sure it doesn't start bleeding again. The liver plays a role in the body's ability to clot."

Hannah made a mental note to check their patient's anticoagulation status as soon as they finished.

"Irrigate the abdominal cavity and let me know when you think we're ready to close."

She nodded and squirted normal saline, watching the surgical tech as she suctioned out the abdomen. When the fluid came back clear, she glanced up at Jake. "I think Mr. Turkow is ready to be closed now."

His gaze over the top of his surgical mask met hers. "I agree. Nice job."

His praise shouldn't mean that much to her, but it did. She was thankful for the fact that her surgical mask covered a good part of her face so he couldn't see how she was blushing.

Jake began closing the abdomen, explaining the different layers as he did the work. When he got to the last layer of skin, he paused and glanced at her. "Do you want to do the final closing?"

She caught her breath. She was so lucky to have this opportunity. "Yes, I would." When he slapped the pick-ups into her hand, she took the instrument and then carefully picked up the needle. Of course her sutures took twice as long as he'd taken to do his, but when she'd finished, she was proud of her work.

She couldn't seem to wipe the smile off her face as they left the surgical suite. She'd assisted with her very first surgery. Hopefully the first of many.

"Hannah?" When Jake called her name, she stopped and glanced back at him over her shoulder. He wasn't smiling.

"Yes?" Her stomach clenched with a sudden attack of nerves and she had to work hard to make sure none of her uncertainty showed on her face.

"Could I have a word with you?" he asked, stripping off his surgical mask and throwing it into the nearest trash can.

"Ah, sure. Of course." Her stomach tightened as she finished washing up at the sink, her mind spinning with possibilities. What on earth did he want to talk to her about? Their night together? The way she'd sneaked out on him? Was he still holding a grudge about that?

Or was this professional? Had she done something wrong in the O.R. that he hadn't wanted to point out in front of the rest of the team? The anesthesiologist had remained in the room, along with the scrub nurse and circulating nurse, for the entire case.

"This way," he murmured, taking her arm and steering her toward the surgeons' lounge. Her nervousness spiked upward several notches when he shut the door behind them for privacy.

When he just stood there, staring at her, she couldn't take the silence. "You were brilliant in there, saving Mr. Turkow's liver like that," she said quickly. "Thanks for giving me the opportunity to assist. I'll gladly close anytime you give me the chance. I'm sure I'll learn a lot from working with you." She knew she was babbling but she couldn't seem to help it.

"Stop it," he said sharply. She sucked in a breath at the flash of anger in his dark chocolate eyes. "You knew exactly who I was when we met down at the marina, so stop acting the part of the starry-eyed intern, grateful for a chance to operate."

"What?" She could feel her cheeks flood with heated embarrassment. Dear God, how could he possibly think she'd engineered their meeting on purpose? Why on earth would she? On her first day of freedom she'd gone sailing on Lake Michigan with her roommate, Margie. Afterward, they'd headed over for a drink at a bar called Shipwrecked. She'd had no idea who Jake was when he'd approached her. The instant physical attraction sizzling between them had been something she'd heard about but never experienced firsthand.

She wished now that she'd ignored him. But she

hadn't. She'd been in a celebratory mood and had flung caution aside to go home with him.

And now they would be forced to work together.

The way he glared at her fueled her temper. "You don't know what you're talking about," she snapped back. "If I recall correctly, you weren't wearing a sign that said Chief of Trauma Surgery: Chicago Care Hospital across your chest when we met. How could I possibly know who you were? Today was my very first day taking care of patients."

"I'm sure you recognized me from the welcome reception on Friday night," he said, refusing to give an inch. "I don't blame you for wanting to advance your career, but, really, sleeping with me was a bit over the top, don't you think?"

Horrified, she gaped at him. He was serious! He actually thought she'd planned the whole thing? Talk about having a healthy ego. "No, in fact, I wasn't able to attend the welcome reception. But you know what? I'm sorry I didn't because if I had attended the reception I would have known exactly who you were and I could have avoided this embarrassment altogether. Trust me, if I had one inkling of who you were, I would never have, you know…" She stopped her frantic babbling with an effort. Enough already!

There was no way to salvage this. Better to just move forward from here, find some way to regain a sense of professionalism.

"You really expect me to believe you didn't know who I was?" he asked in a skeptical tone.

She lifted her chin. She hadn't gotten this far in her career without the ability to stand up for herself. "You can believe whatever you want, Dr. Holt," she said coolly. "It doesn't matter to me one way or the other. As far as I'm concerned, we can pretend that unfortunate situation never happened." His eyes narrowed as if her comment stung. Hanging on to her composure wasn't easy. "I worked really hard to earn a spot in this residency, and I will not do anything to mess that up. So are we clear on that subject? Or do we need to beat it to death some more?"

The flash of uncertainty in his gaze gave her a small sense of satisfaction. And for a moment she desperately wished things could be different. If only Jake wasn't so darned gorgeous. And sexy. And the damn freaking chief of trauma surgery! Of all the guys to fall into bed with, she'd had to pick this one! Trust her to screw up her last night of freedom. No pun intended.

He lifted a shoulder, as if he didn't care one way or the other. "Fine. Consider the night forgotten."

The sudden sense of loss caught her off guard. For some reason she was thoroughly annoyed he'd given in so easily.

Of course, this was exactly what she wanted. Right? Right. She forced a tight smile. "Thank you."

"Anytime."

She frowned and narrowed her gaze. Was that a sexual innuendo? No, of course it wasn't. He was just being nice. Polite. Professional.

She pasted a smile on her face and turned to make her way to the lounge door. Time to put this entire incident behind her once and for all.

"Dr. Stewart?" Once again, his voice stopped her.

The formal way he addressed her was slightly reassuring. She had to stop being suspicious about every conversation. After all, they were going to be spending the entire month together. A very long month. No doubt he wanted to ask her something about their patient. "Yes?"

"I have a firm rule about never dating anyone I work with, so I truly hope you're going to be professional about this."

Oh, he had a rule, did he? Well, good. Being an intern was all about following rules. And why on earth did he think she wouldn't be professional? His gall was too much. "Of course. Is there anything else? If not, I'm going to check on Mr. Turkow."

"No, that's all."

His dismissive tone grated on her nerves. She headed back to the locker room, more disturbed by his parting comment than she wanted to admit. She opened her locker and retrieved her lab coat, slamming the door with more force than was necessary.

Why was she suddenly feeling as if she was the one who'd stepped out of line? As if this entire mess was her fault and her fault only? As if he hadn't participated one little bit?

Their night together had been more his idea than hers. He'd been the one to approach *her*. He'd been the one to take her hand, hauling her from the bar. Granted, she hadn't exactly fought him off, but still.

He was the one who'd suggested they go to his place! And like a fool, she'd tossed common sense aside to go with him.

Experiencing the most incredible night of passion she'd ever had in her life.

For a moment she rested her heated forehead on the cool metal locker. Their night together had affected her more than she'd realized. But she needed to get over it.

She had to follow Jake's example and strive to remain professional.

She'd worked too damn hard—served countless drinks, endured hundreds of passes, cleaned endless offices and studied for thousands of hours—to get where she was today.

As far as she was concerned, Dr. Jake Holt could pick someone else to scorch with his good looks.

CHAPTER THREE

ASSAILED by a truckload of doubt, Jake stared at the lounge door that remained closed behind Hannah, fighting the insane urge to go after her.

Had he really been wrong about her?

The horror in her eyes had been too real to be faked. And the confrontation hadn't gone at all the way he'd thought it would. She'd stood up to him. Tossed his accusations back at him. And she hadn't thrown herself into his arms, begging for forgiveness.

The way Allie had, once he'd discovered her true motives for going out with him.

No, Hannah had almost looked hurt. Claiming that if she'd known who he was, she wouldn't have gone anywhere near him. And he'd sensed that much at least was the truth.

The desolate sense of loss surprised him.

He took a deep breath and shoved the wave of self-doubt aside. Did it really matter if Hannah was telling the truth? No, because that fact changed nothing. She was still an intern in the residency program and he was still the chief of trauma surgery.

He'd learned the hard way, thanks to Allie, the perils of dating someone who worked at the same hospital.

Someone you were forced to see almost every day. Where everyone knew everyone else's business.

If he'd been smart, he would have left Minneapolis a long time ago. But he'd refused to run away. He'd taken this job because it was a promotion. Not because he couldn't take the constant churning of the rumor mill.

In the privacy of the lounge, he let down his guard and scrubbed his hands over his face. Flirting with Hannah, buying her a drink and then spending the night with her had been completely out of character. He knew a good portion of the reason he'd acted so impulsively was due to his sheer determination to make a fresh start.

A new career in a new city, and a steadfast resolve to leave his old baggage behind once and for all. Recklessly, he'd responded to the instant attraction he'd felt with Hannah. Seeing her sailing, and meeting her at the lakeshore bar, he'd never imagined she might be connected to the hospital in some way. And he'd been secretly thrilled when she'd agreed to go home with him. They'd shared an incredible night together.

His intention of putting his past behind him and moving forward had backfired in a big way. Somehow, he'd only managed to complicate his life even further, by sleeping with his intern.

With a sigh, Jake stood and stalked out of the lounge. There was no reason to dwell on the mistake he'd made with Hannah. The more he thought about it, the more he realized she'd likely remain professional. After all, she'd been the one to sneak out that morning.

And she'd also insisted they act as if their night together had never happened.

Maybe her ability to brush him aside annoyed the hell out of him, but he was determined to remain thankful she wasn't clinging to some ridiculous romantic notion that they were meant to be together forever.

He'd gone down that path with Allie, only to discover he couldn't have been more wrong. After swearing off women, he'd opened his heart to Allie, only to have it ripped from his chest and stomped on. He'd managed to put his life back on track, although it hadn't been easy.

No matter how attracted he'd been to Hannah, he wasn't about to get hurt or be made a fool of ever again.

Satisfied that he'd wrenched Hannah out of his system, he headed to the recovery area to check on Mr. Turkow. Of course, Hannah was there, poring over the patient's lab work. Trying to ignore her was harder than he'd anticipated, seemingly aware of every breath she took as he quickly reviewed their patient's vitals for himself.

"He looks stable," Hannah said. "Do you want him to go to a regular surgical floor or the ICU?"

"Definitely the ICU. You'll need to keep a close eye on him as the next few hours are critical. He could easily continue bleeding or come down with an infection."

"Understood," Hannah agreed. He shouldn't have been annoyed at her level of professionalism. "Do you want me to write the admission orders?"

He nodded, knowing he'd have time to review the orders himself, later. "And make sure to call me if there are any significant changes or if you need something."

"Of course. I'm on call tonight, so I'll be able to check him frequently."

He froze. What? She was the intern on call to-night?

Perfect. That was just perfect. Because he was the attending on call tonight, too.

Did he have a black cloud hanging over his head, or what?

His pager went off. Grateful for the interruption, he glanced down to read the message from Richard, who was requesting his help in the O.R. "I have to go," he said, avoiding Hannah's gaze. "I'll be in the O.R. if you need anything."

As he scrubbed in, he couldn't help thinking about how he'd be forced to spend the entire night with Hannah. One of the first changes he'd made as the new chief of trauma was to require that the attending physicians stayed in-house 24/7. His colleagues hadn't been thrilled with the new requirement, but he knew that having the attending physicians readily available for trauma resuscitations and for emergency surgeries would improve their patients' outcomes. He'd been brought in to make sure Chicago Care didn't lose its precarious level-one trauma verification, which was scheduled to be reviewed in just six weeks. This was the first step toward reaching that goal.

So he'd made the decision and had agreed to do the first week of call. In fact, he'd taken the first week and the last week in July to be on call, since it was their busiest month with trauma patients.

Drying his hands on the sterile towels the circulating nurse provided, the impact of his decision hit him squarely in the chest. Two weeks of call in July meant he'd be working with Hannah often.

Too often.

Since avoiding her would be next to impossible,

he'd have lots of practice keeping their relationship professional.

With grim determination, he could only hope he'd succeed in that goal, too.

Hannah couldn't believe how fast her day went. Overall she thought she'd done fairly well in keeping things on a cool, professional level with Jake.

Dr. Holt. She really needed to start thinking of him as Dr. Holt.

She'd given Mr. Turkow another two units of blood and his condition had stabilized nicely. She'd also given the orders for the nurses to wean Mr. Turkow from the ventilator after she'd verified that his lungs were fully inflated following his pneumothorax. When it was time to extubate him, she called Jake just to make sure she was on the right track. Jake had immediately come up to the ICU to review everything she'd done for the patient, before agreeing with her plan.

"You'll need to be ready to make rounds with me in fifteen minutes," he said in a curt tone.

"Rounds?" she repeated, a little confused. Generally the surgical teams made rounds first thing in the morning. Not five o'clock in the evening.

He looked her straight in the eye. "You said you're taking first call tonight, right?" When she nodded, he continued, "I'm the attending on call tonight as well and we need to see every patient on service so you understand my expectations."

Oka-a-a-y, now she understood. Wasn't it just her luck that he was the attending on call? As if it wasn't difficult enough working with him during the day? She made sure her dismay didn't show. "Of course. Do you want to meet in the ICU first?" Logically, she thought starting with the sickest patients made the most sense.

"No, we'll start on the general surgical floor. The ICU patients are going to take longer to review as their medical needs are more complicated, so I generally leave them for last."

She took a deep breath and nodded. So much for her logic. She felt as if she was fighting an uphill battle to earn Jake's respect as a physician. Refusing to let her nervousness show, Hannah pulled out her new pack of three-by-five note cards and prepared to take good notes. As a medical student she'd learned the trick of putting each patient on a card and using them as a reference throughout the night.

Although this was the first time she'd be the one responsible for making the medical decisions. Decisions that Jake would use as a basis to critique her performance. She ignored a flutter of panic.

Actually, it was good news that the attending surgeon, even if it was Jake, would be in house all night. At least she would have backup if she got in over her head. For some reason, every time she looked for Richard, the senior resident, he was busy elsewhere.

She would have felt completely alone if not for Jake.

After copying Mr. Turkow's information on a card, she hurried out to the general trauma surgical floor to meet Jake. *Dr. Holt.*

She should have been glad that he treated her like any other resident in the program, but as they made rounds on the patients, talking to the nurses and reviewing their charts, she couldn't seem to stop searching his gaze for some sign of—what? She didn't really know.

Recognition? Acknowledgement? Support? Cama-raderie?

What she got was indifferent professionalism.

He was right that the ICU patients took much longer to do rounds on. When they finished, she had a thick stack of cards with key information for each patient noted on them.

"Dr. Holt, could you tell me where the trauma-surgery call rooms are located?" she asked. She'd learned during the tour earlier that morning that each service had a group of call rooms, but she'd lost track of exactly which ones were located where.

He raised a brow. "Do you honestly think you're going to be spending much time in your call room?" he asked with a note of sarcasm.

"No," she answered candidly. "But I'd still like to know where they are, just in case by some miracle I am able to get one or two hours of sleep tonight."

The corner of his mouth tipped upward in a half smile and she was grateful for the tiny crack of humanity beneath the layer of cool professionalism.

She much preferred Jake the man over Dr. Holt the chief of trauma surgery.

Get used to it, she reminded herself. From here on out, she was only working with Dr. Holt, the chief of trauma surgery. Jake the man didn't exist.

Not for her. Not anymore.

"First floor, west corridor down the hall from the trauma bays," he said. "You can pick up a key for the call rooms from the operator."

"Thanks." She was starving, having only eaten a handful of crackers from the ICU kitchenette for lunch, so she quickly ran down to get her key from the operator and then headed over to the cafeteria.

Apparently Jake had the same idea, to eat now before something bad happened, because he arrived as she was waiting for her chicken sandwich and fries. She saw him come up beside her out of the corner of her eye. She tried not to breathe in too deeply the familiar, musky scent of his aftershave.

A stirring of desire flickered low in her belly. She did her best to ignore it. Cripes, she really needed to get past this insane physical response to the man.

She quickly paid for her meal and then desperately glanced around the cafeteria for someplace to sit. She saw the familiar face of one of the other interns from her group, and quickly read his name tag. Kyle Franklin. "Hey, do you mind if I eat with you?"

"No problem," Kyle said, waving a hand at the empty seat.

She sat down gratefully. "So what service did you end up on?" she asked conversationally.

"Ob-gyn," he muttered with a grimace. "How about you?"

"Trauma," she answered.

"Damn, you're lucky. Summer is the best time to be on trauma. Of course, I'm not on the trauma service until November. Boring." He took a bite of his pizza and then groaned when his pager went off. He glanced down at it with annoyance. "Great. A woman just arrived in active labor. Sorry to cut this short but I gotta go." He shoved the last bit of pizza into his mouth and then took off running.

Alone again, Hannah sighed and took a bite of her

chicken sandwich. She tensed when a familiar scent teased her senses.

"Do you mind if I sit down?" Jake asked.

The mouthful of food lodged in her throat and she had to take a sip of her water to prevent herself choking. Was he doing this on purpose? Why on earth had he chosen to come over to sit with her? On the other hand, how did you say no to the chief of trauma? "Ah, no, I don't mind," she managed. She set down her water with a jerky movement that almost upended the cup. "Dr. Franklin had to leave for a delivery."

"You need to relax," he advised, as he plunked his tray on the table across from her.

Relax? Was he kidding?

"You were tense all through rounds," he pointed out, after taking a healthy bite of his burger. "Since you can't seem to relax while working with me, I'd be happy to support a request for you to transfer off Trauma."

Transfer off Trauma? She stared at him in horror. Was that even an option? But she narrowed her gaze when she noted the flicker of hope in his eyes. Oh, sure, he'd love her to transfer off Trauma, wouldn't he? That would be a ridiculously easy way to get rid of her. Well, fat chance. Kyle was right—summer was the best time to be on Trauma. No way was she going to admit defeat. "I'm not tense, just excited," she said, stretching the truth just a bit. "Being on Trauma is a total thrill. I've done more procedures today than general-surgery interns do in a week."

"You might change your mind after working thirty hours straight," he said, as if surprised by her response.

Keeping the easy smile on her face wasn't easy,

considering she knew how incredible he looked naked.

Stop it! She had to stop thinking about that.

She shrugged. "It's all part of the package, right? I pulled plenty of all-nighters during medical school, so it won't be anything new." He had no idea how she'd struggled to juggle two jobs along with the responsibilities of being on service as a third- and fourth-year med student. "I know the hours are long and the pay is dismal but I'm totally psyched to learn everything I can."

"The pay won't be dismal forever," he murmured.

She remembered his chrome and glass condo decor and decided there was no reason to be rude. "I know. But, really, it doesn't matter. I've always worked hard and at least now I'm doing something I truly enjoy." And nothing, especially not a sexy attending physician, was going to stop her.

"Oh, yeah?" He lifted a curious gaze. "What did you used to do?"

She blanched and stared at her fries for a second. "Oh, you know, the usual low-paying jobs to get through college," she said evasively.

"Did you grow up around here?"

Uh-oh, now he was treading on dangerous ground. She didn't want anyone to know the details of the life she'd worked hard to leave behind. Especially not Jake. *Dr. Holt.* "Er…no, not really." She'd grown up in a galaxy far, far away. Or so it seemed. Time to change the subject. "But I have to say, it's amazing how Chicago Care is so close to the lake. I just love watching the sun rise over Lake Michigan in the mornings. I don't think I'll ever tire of the sight."

For a long moment, his dark gaze pierced hers and

suddenly she knew he was remembering their morning together. Had it been just two days ago? Seemed like much longer.

Another lifetime. For a nanosecond, she wished they could go back to simply being the two people attracted to each other who'd met at the bar.

"Yes, the view of the lake is spectacular," he agreed. Was the husky note in his tone her imagination? Probably.

They were professionals. Working together. That's all.

Her pager went off and she was grateful for the interruption. "This is the surgical ICU calling. Sorry, but I need to go."

"Why don't you call them first to see what they want?" he asked. "You might not need to sacrifice the rest of your meal."

She needed to get away from him, for many reasons, but most of all her sanity. She jumped on the excuse to leave. "It's a text page about Mr. Turkow's blood pressure—it's down. I need to run up and examine him."

Jake frowned and nodded. "All right. Call me if you need me," he said. "I'll be by to check on him later."

"Of course." As if there was any other option? He was the boss, after all. She took one last bite of her chicken sandwich and then hauled her tray to the sideboard, feeling his gaze on her back as she left.

She let out a sigh of relief when she stepped into the elevator to head up to the third floor. She could do this. Work with Jake as a professional.

She had no choice but to do this.

* * *

By midnight, Hannah had lost count of the number of pages she received. Thank God for her note cards because she'd responded to some issue on almost every patient on their service and she'd never have been able to keep track of the patients without her notes.

As Jake had predicted, she didn't even see the inside of her call room until two in the morning. She stretched out on the bed and closed her eyes. One hour. She desperately needed one hour of peace and quiet.

At two forty-five, her pager went off, announcing the arrival of a new trauma patient. Overall, the night had been quiet as far as trauma calls went. But maybe the trauma activity only started to heat up in the wee hours of the morning.

The responsibility of being a doctor seemed almost overwhelming. Yet this was something she'd dreamed about for years. Ever since she'd been hospitalized with a ruptured appendix at the age of thirteen. Her surgeon, Dr. Marilee McDaniel, had been amazing. After a week in the hospital, Hannah had vowed to be just like her.

The hardships would be worth it. Hannah rolled out of bed and splashed some water on her face in a pathetic attempt to wipe away the fatigue. Forty-five minutes was almost an hour, wasn't it?

Of course it was.

She headed down to the trauma bay, only to find Jake already there, standing at the patient's bedside. He didn't look nearly as tired as she felt.

"What do we have?" she asked in a low voice.

"A young man with Ehlers-Danlos syndrome." Jake glanced up at her. "Are you familiar with it?"

Ehlers-Danlos syndrome? She stared at him. Her mind went blank. Absolutely, completely blank.

"No?" The sharp disappointment in his tone hurt, more than it should have. "I suggest you do some research—it's a rare genetic disorder."

She glanced over at the patient, a very handsome young man who looked to be in his early twenties. He was moaning and grimacing, as if he was in excruciating pain.

"Start a dilaudid pain pump and get a full-body CT scan," Jake said to the nurse. "And I want to see the results of his CT scan, stat."

Hannah pushed the emotionally draining exhaustion away and forced herself to focus. She had read about the disease, she knew she had. As she and Jake stepped away from the bedside, she finally pulled the knowledge from the deep recesses of her brain. "Ehlers-Danlos syndrome is classified by weak tissue, primarily blood vessels, resulting in multiple aneurysms."

"Yes." There was a flash of approval in Jake's gaze. But then he turned serious again. "Unfortunately, Christopher Melbourne was first diagnosed with this disease at the age of seven."

Seven? Good heavens, she couldn't even imagine. "It's a miracle he's survived this long," she murmured.

"Yes. Although with the abdominal pain he's currently experiencing, I'm very much afraid he has a leaking abdominal aortic aneurysm."

Her stomach clenched. Abdominal aortic aneurysms were known to be serious, life-threatening conditions. "Can you surgically repair it?"

"No. Too risky. All his blood vessels are weak and fragile, to the point that they would never hold a new tissue graft. As it is, he's been walking around with a large aneurysm in his axillary artery that no surgeon has been brave enough to repair."

They couldn't operate? "So what can we do for him?"

Jake slowly shook his head, and she caught a surprising glimpse of true anguish in his eyes.

"Nothing. Except make him as comfortable as possible until he dies."

CHAPTER FOUR

JAKE stared at the dismal results of Christopher's CT scan, battling a surge of helplessness. He'd never seen an abdominal aneurysm this huge, extending from the heart all the way down to the kidneys. He was amazed Christopher was still coherent. No way could he afford to operate on this poor kid. He'd die on the O.R. table for sure.

There was nothing worse than losing a young patient.

Except maybe standing by and doing nothing while watching him die.

He scrubbed a hand over his jaw and sighed. No matter how much he wished otherwise, there wasn't a single treatment option he could offer. Except comfort measures. He walked back to Christopher's bedside where Hannah was finishing her head-to-toe assessment. "I've confirmed a leaking triple A," he said in a low tone, not meant for Christopher to hear. "We need to get him transferred up to the surgical ICU."

"Doctor...have you...called my father?" Christopher asked Hannah, his wide eyes sunken into his thin face.

Hannah leaned over and took Christopher's frail hand

firmly in hers. As they'd worked together over the past several hours, Jake had noticed she touched patients a lot. Connecting in a way that made them trust her. If she kept up the way she was going, she'd be a great surgeon. "Yes, he's on his way."

"Good," Christopher whispered, before closing his eyes on another wave of pain.

Hannah brought her tortured gaze up to meet Jake's and he slowly shook his head at her unspoken question. If he could somehow pull off a miracle, he would. But Christopher was dying. The boy's fate was no longer in his hands.

Just as they were about to wheel him up to the ICU, his father, Allen Melbourne, rushed in, eyes wide with fear. "Chris? Are you okay?"

"Dad," Chris whispered, reaching out for his father. "I'm glad you're here. The pain is bad. Really bad."

Jake saw the question in the father's eyes and has-tened to assure him. "We have him on a pain pump, with a substantial dose of the strongest narcotic we have. He should start to feel better soon. And we're moving him to the ICU."

"Not to surgery?" Allen asked with a frown, glancing between Jake and Hannah.

"No. I'm afraid Chris isn't a candidate for surgery," Jake said, as gently as he could. At this point Chris was technically a full code, but Jake had no plans to actively resuscitate him. In fact, he shouldn't really take him to the ICU, but he wanted Chris and his father to know he'd be closely watched.

Myriad emotions played over Allen's face until, eventually, resigned acceptance remained. Jake noticed

Hannah's eyes glistening with tears, but then she quickly pulled herself under control.

"We're going to take very good care of your son," she promised.

"I know," Allen said simply. He held his son's hand as they wheeled him down the hall toward the elevators. The simple ride to the third floor seemed excruciatingly long.

Within ten minutes of their arrival in the ICU, however, Christopher's monitor began to alarm, signaling dangerously low blood pressure. Seconds later, his heart slowed down.

"We're losing him," Hannah said urgently. "Get the crash cart!" And before he could stop her, she jumped up on the edge of the bed and began performing chest compressions.

On the third stroke downward, a large crack echoed through the room. For one horrified moment everyone froze, realizing Hannah had broken several of Christopher's ribs.

"Stop!" Allen cried, as the monitor continued to beep. "No more! That's enough."

Hannah stumbled to the floor and backed away from the bed, her eyes revealing her acute devastation. Jake wanted to reassure her that she hadn't done anything wrong. Surely she knew breaking ribs was a common complication of doing CPR? But it was possible she'd never experienced it herself.

Sometimes being a doctor sucked.

Allen held his son close and sobbed as Christopher's heart rate continued to slow and then eventually stopped. The nurse, thankfully, had turned off the annoying monitor alarm.

Without warning, Hannah whirled and ran from the room. Jake wanted to go after her, but he needed to finish here first.

"Mr. Melbourne, I'm sorry for your loss," he murmured. Losing a patient was the hardest part of being a surgeon. A surgeon's mentality was to believe they could fix anything. And a good portion of the time, that was true. But not always. Like now. "I need to know if you want us to do an autopsy so we can confirm what caused Chris's death."

Allen shook his head, his eyes red-rimmed and full of tears. "You already know what caused him to die, don't you? A ruptured aneurysm. No, I don't want an autopsy."

Jake didn't blame him, but they were required to ask. And in the case of Ehlers-Danlos syndrome, there might be something they could learn from the rare hereditary disease. But he didn't have the heart to push. "It's your choice," he said. "Again, I'm sorry for your loss."

"Thank you," Allen muttered, before bending over his son one last time. The nurse shut off the monitor and the IV pumps as Jake finished the death paperwork that would normally be the responsibility of the residents.

He left the ICU and paused outside the elevator. He was exhausted, but he knew he wouldn't be able to rest until he'd checked on Hannah.

With a resigned sigh, he headed down to the trauma-residency call rooms.

His call room was located on the other side of the building, near the faculty offices, but he made it his business to know where the residents would be sleeping, in case he needed to drag one of them out of bed. He hesitated in front of the call room assigned to the first-year trauma resident, second-guessing his decision to come here. Half-tempted to leave her alone, he heard it. The unmistakable sound of muffled crying.

"Hannah?" He knocked sharply on the door, knowing he couldn't leave her like that. "It's me. Jake. Open up."

He heard her sniffle and then blow her nose, before she finally opened the door. The sight of her tear-streaked face made him want to pull her close in spite of his determination to keep his distance.

She didn't invite him in, didn't say anything at all as she stood there, until he finally asked, "Are you all right?"

"I'm fine." Her expression was brittle and he sensed she was hanging on by a thread. "I'm sorry, I know I shouldn't have let my emotions get the better of me, leaving you alone like that. If you give me a few minutes, I'll go back upstairs to finish the paperwork."

"I already took care of it." He stepped forward, forcing the issue, and she moved backward, allowing him to come in. After another long silence, he finally spoke. "It's my fault, you know."

That shocked her. "What do you mean?"

He sighed. "I had no intention of coding that young man. Doing CPR, giving drugs, none of that was going to work when he was literally bleeding to death. But I should have told you the plan."

She bit her lip and her beautiful blue eyes filled again with tears. "I broke his ribs," she murmured with an anguished cry. "I promised we'd take care of him and instead I broke his ribs!"

"Hannah, please." He couldn't stand watching her

beat herself up for something that really was his fault. "You know it's a risk of CPR."

She nodded, but then her eyes filled with tears. She turned away, covering her face with her hands.

There were a lot of things he could have said. He could have assured her that it's never easy for any doctor to lose a patient. That some deaths, like Christopher's, were inevitable.

But he didn't say any of those things. Instead, he reached out and pulled her firmly into his arms. At first she resisted, but he didn't let go.

After a heartbeat, she collapsed against him, burying her face in the hollow of his shoulder. He held her and murmured nonsense in her ear, as she struggled to bring her emotions under control.

Finally, the tears stopped and the tension eased from her shoulders.

And despite the sad and unfortunate circumstances that had brought them together, all he could think about was how right Hannah felt in his arms.

And how much he didn't want to let her go.

Hannah instantly regretted the moment of weakness. She shouldn't have given in to her turbulent emotions, brought on, no doubt, by her bone-weary exhaustion. But the loud crack of the broken ribs kept echoing over and over in her mind. And that, coupled with how Christopher's father had cried and held his son, had just been too much.

She hadn't seen her own father in years. Since she was ten. And she couldn't imagine he'd ever cried a day in his life. Especially not over the family he'd abandoned without a backward glance.

Dwelling on her family issues wouldn't help, so she pushed them aside and tried to pull herself together. This wasn't the first patient she'd lost. And undoubtedly wouldn't be the last.

But with Jake's arms holding her close, his familiar musky scent filling her senses, she couldn't find the energy to break away.

Being with him felt right. How was it possible that she actually missed him? Missed being held by him? Totally ridiculous, considering she'd only first met him a couple of days ago.

She took a deep breath, intending to pull away. Being close to Jake wasn't healthy. He was her boss, after all. Besides, if she wanted to be taken seriously as a surgeon she couldn't fall apart every time she lost a patient.

But then he stroked his hand slowly, deliberately down her back, and she shivered. In a moment the embrace morphed from something nice and comforting to sizzling sexual awareness. Instinctively, she pressed more firmly against him.

He nuzzled the sensitive hollow behind her ear, an erogenous zone she hadn't even known she possessed. She shivered again and gasped, every atom in her body longing for more.

"Hannah," he murmured, just moments before his mouth claimed hers in an explosive kiss.

It was a replay that mirrored the first night when he'd kissed her on the elevator ride up to his condo.

And just like then, she was powerless to resist. He made love to her with his mouth, his tongue probing deep, and she urged him back against the wall, tugging his scrub shirt upward so she could rake her hands up and over his chest.

When she tugged at the knot in the ties of his scrub pants, she could feel the hard urgency of his erection straining against the thin fabric. She slowly stroked him.

Jake stiffened and thrust against her hand, but then abruptly broke off the kiss and tore himself away. She stumbled backward and for a dazed moment stared at him, struggling to breathe, trying to figure out what was wrong.

"We can't do this," he said in a harsh tone. His erratic breathing matched hers as he straightened his scrubs. She was somewhat glad to know his body had wanted her, even if his mind didn't.

"But—" She stopped, as reality set in. Of course they couldn't do this. He was her boss. And she wasn't the person he thought she was. She'd never fit into his world.

No matter how much she wanted to. Wanted him.

"No, Hannah. This isn't going to happen. This won't happen ever again!" The edge of desperation in his tone made her wonder who he was trying so hard to convince. Her? Or himself? But then it didn't matter because he wrenched open her door and stalked out, slamming it shut behind him.

She winced and collapsed on her narrow cot, threading her fingers through her hair in a gesture of helplessness. Well. That certainly could have gone better.

And even though she knew, logically, he was right to stop before things really got out of control, she also couldn't help resenting the hell out of him. Because he'd been the one to break off the embrace. It would have been far better if she could have been the strong one, but deep down she knew she didn't have the strength to push him away.

Might never have the strength to push him away.

Mulling over that sobering thought, her pager went off for the zillionth time. She dialed the phone, knowing that somehow, impossible as the task seemed, she needed to figure out a way to keep her distance from Jake Holt.

The next morning, Hannah took a shower in the women's locker room, trying to wash away the fatigue that seemed to coat her skin.

Thanks to Jake's kiss, she'd lost the one measly hour of sleep she could have had.

Damn the man, anyway. Why had he come down to her call room? She would have pulled herself together.

Over the course of her life, she'd managed far more adversity than this. And had always found a way to get through it.

As she was tying the drawstring on a pair of clean scrubs, Andrea came into the locker room. "Well?" Andrea demanded anxiously. "How was it? Rough?"

It took a moment for Hannah to realize Andrea wasn't asking about Jake's kiss in the call room, but how her first night on call had gone. "It was really busy," she answered honestly. "We lost a patient last night and transferred one of our floor patients to the ICU to be treated for septic shock."

"You lost a patient?" Andrea said, her eyes widening in horror. "Oh, you know what that means?"

Hannah sighed as she slid her arms into the sleeves of her lab coat. "Yeah, it means a young man died despite our best efforts to save him."

"No, it means you'll have to present the case at M & M rounds," Andrea corrected.

What? She stared at Andrea, the knot in her stomach tightening painfully. Andrea was right. How on earth could she have forgotten how Dr. Phillips had spoken at their orientation session about a resident's responsibility at their weekly morbidity and mortality rounds? "Oh, no," she whispered, as the implication sank into her brain. "I hadn't thought of that."

"Well, maybe it won't be as bad as what we're imagining," Andrea said reassuringly. "After all, it can't be that unusual to lose patients on the trauma service."

Hannah tucked her stethoscope into her right-hand pocket and then shut her locker. Christopher hadn't died because of anything they had or hadn't done. But M & M rounds were as much about teaching and learning what, if anything, they could have done differently.

During her student days she'd observed enough presentations to know some of the more experienced surgical residents loved to put the new surgical interns on the spot by asking really difficult questions.

She swallowed hard, vowing to brush up on every single aspect of Ehlers-Danlos syndrome. And pray that no one would ask why she'd started CPR and cracked his ribs. The sick feeling in her gut intensified.

"Don't think about it," Andrea advised. "Really, I shouldn't have even brought it up. Even if you do end up presenting your case, it probably won't happen until next week. You'll have plenty of time to prepare."

She nodded, knowing that a few days didn't matter much in the big scheme of things. Hannah made a mental note to ask Jake about it later. She'd rather ask one of the other attendings, but Jake happened to be the one on service when Christopher had died. For now, they had to hustle or they'd be late for rounds.

Jake was waiting for them in the central nurses' station on the general-surgery floor. Hannah couldn't help noticing the way he avoided her gaze when she and Andrea walked up to join the group of residents who'd already gathered there.

When the last resident, Dave Harrison, hurried in, Jake frowned and glanced pointedly at his watch. "You're late," he said flatly.

"Sorry, Dr. Holt," Dave said earnestly. "Traffic was awful."

Jake's scowl deepened. "This is Chicago, Harrison. Traffic is always awful. Get your butt out of bed earlier."

Dave flushed and nodded. "Yessir."

Hannah felt bad for Dave, yet at the same time she was relieved to know that she and Andrea hadn't been the last ones to arrive. Better for her if she could manage to stay on Jake's good side.

If she hadn't ruined that chance already.

"All right, we have twelve patients to do rounds on today, so let's get going. We're going to start with Mr. Anderson, in room twenty-three."

Jake strode down the hall toward Mr. Anderson's room and they all hurried to keep up with him. As she'd been the one on call and covering all night, she knew that Jake was going to ask how things had gone so she pulled out her three-by-five note cards and began thumbing through them.

Mr. Anderson's nurse joined them outside his room. Hannah quickly filled in the rest of the residents on how the patient's finger-stick glucoses had been running higher than normal so she'd increased the amount of insulin he was getting. Jake nodded, agreeing with her actions, and then directed most of his questions to the nurse. "Make sure he gets out of bed to walk today," he said sternly, before heading to the next room.

Hannah's relief was short-lived. She soon learned that every single order she'd written while being on call the night before was reviewed and rehashed not just by Jake but by the rest of the team.

Thankfully, for the most part everything she'd done for the general-floor patients was deemed appropriate. So they moved on to the ICU to look at the sicker patients.

Jake headed to Mr. Turkow's bedside first. This time she didn't need her note cards, because she was intimately familiar with the case.

"He was weaned off the vent last evening and had a good night," Hannah said as Jake logged on to the computer. "His labs are stable, there's no sign of bleeding. I think he can probably be transferred to the regular surgical floor today."

"Hmm," Jake murmured, his gaze focused on the computer screen where he reviewed Mr. Turkow's detailed medical information. "Dr. Stewart, do you want to explain why you ordered a subtherapeutic dose of antibiotics for this patient?"

Sub-therapeutic? She frowned, trying to remember what she'd ordered. "I ordered a hundred and ninety milligrams of Zithromax when his cultures came back last evening."

"He's only on a hundred milligrams of Zithromax," Jake corrected sharply. "You ordered the wrong dose and you're lucky the patient hasn't suffered an adverse effect as a result."

"I didn't order the wrong dose," she responded defensively, her cheeks burning with acute embarrassment. She specifically remembered looking up the antibiotic to make sure she was ordering the correct dose. She grabbed Mr. Turkow's chart and flipped open to the antibiotic order form. Her heart sank when she realized what happened.

Her writing had been sloppy and the nine had been mistaken by both the nurse and the pharmacist for a zero. She'd written the order as she'd been receiving a page about another patient and had rushed through it.

"I…can see the wrong dose was entered in error. I wrote for the correct dose of one hundred and ninety milligrams, but the nurse and the pharmacist both thought the order was for one hundred milligrams."

"Next time, make sure your orders are clear, Dr. Stewart," Jake said bluntly, his expression hard, as if those moments between them in the call room had never happened. Or maybe he was punishing her for that kiss. "Sloppiness can kill a patient and will not be tolerated. Understand?"

Numbly she nodded. Jake had made it perfectly clear that not only was there nothing personal between them but that she'd have to work harder than anyone else in order to earn his respect on a professional level.

She couldn't afford the smallest mistake if she wanted to succeed in this program.

CHAPTER FIVE

MAYBE he'd been a little too hard on her, Jake thought with a twinge of regret as he watched Hannah leave the ICU after they'd finished rounds. For a split second he considered going after her, but then the logical side of his mind quickly overruled the emotional impulse.

Following Hannah was exactly what had got him in trouble earlier that morning. Going to her call room because he'd known she was upset had been incredibly stupid. Taking her into his arms to offer comfort had been even worse. How on earth he'd managed to pull away from her, when he'd wanted nothing more than to make love with her again, he'd never know.

Over the past twenty-four hours they'd worked together, he'd realized she couldn't have set him up at the bar. For one thing, no one had known his plans to accompany Gregory Matthews on his yacht for the day. Plus, he'd asked his administrative assistant to check the welcome-reception list and discovered Hannah had, in fact, declined the invitation. Yet in the moment in her call room, when she'd responded so passionately to his kiss, the flash of doubt had returned.

If she hadn't known who he was a few days ago, she certainly did now. And he couldn't ignore the possibility she was still interested in using the physical attraction between them to advance her career.

He needed to stop caring about her on a personal level. If Hannah was upset by having her mistakes pointed out to her, she shouldn't have applied to a competitive surgical residency program. And she'd better grow a thicker skin.

Patient care was his priority. Every doctor in the hospital had to learn from their mistakes. The sooner she realized that, the better. She was no different from anyone else.

And maybe if he told himself that ten more times he'd find a way to believe it.

Pushing away thoughts of Hannah, he glanced at his watch as he headed back down to the trauma bay. His shift would officially end when he reported off to the next attending, and since a trauma call had come in a few minutes ago, he knew his colleague, Steven White, would be there. Jake was still on call for the rest of the week, so he'd be due back for evening rounds at five-thirty.

Not much time off work, but enough to run home, maybe hit the gym for a few hours before coming back to the hospital.

When he poked his head into the trauma bay, he frowned when he saw Hannah there, standing off to the side, watching a patient being resuscitated from what appeared to be a cardiac arrest.

"What are you still doing here, Dr. Stewart?" he asked in a low voice so as not to disturb the staff running the code blue under the direction of Steven White.

She didn't even glance at him. "Observing."

Her tart tone made him grind his teeth in frustration.

He could see that much for himself, but what he didn't understand was why. "Residency rules require that you leave the hospital by noon on the days you're post-call."

"I'm aware of the residency rules, Dr. Holt," she murmured, her gaze glued to the staff working on the patient. "And in case you haven't noticed, it's not quite noon yet. I have fifteen minutes to observe."

Fifteen minutes. He couldn't believe what he was hearing. Hannah had to be exhausted. He knew she hadn't had much sleep last night. Hell, he'd only managed a total of four hours himself, and he hadn't been first call. It seemed ridiculous to stand around observing when she could be at home, asleep. Was she really this dedicated to learning? Or was she simply putting on a good show for the attending physician's benefit?

For his benefit?

"Your dedication to learning is duly noted, but your shift is over, Dr. Stewart. Go home."

She glanced pointedly at the clock and then focused her attention back on the CPR efforts of the trauma staff. Her unspoken message was clear. She would leave the hospital when required and not one minute sooner.

He couldn't explain why her defiance annoyed him so much. "If you're doing this for my sake, don't bother. You won't get extra-credit points from me."

That comment finally broke through her wall of indifference and she turned on him, her blue eyes glittering with icy frost. "I'm observing this resuscitation effort for my sake, not yours. And I fail to see why you care how I spend my time, Dr. Holt."

He slammed a lid on his temper with an effort. "I don't care how you spend your time," he said, even though it was a blatant lie, because for some strange reason he did care. Far more than he should. "But I'm responsible for making sure our residents follow the eighty-hour work rule. I refuse to allow you or anyone else to jeopardize our program."

"I won't jeopardize your program," she said flatly, turning away.

Maybe, maybe not. He crossed his arms over his chest and waited beside her, as he couldn't interrupt his colleague in the middle of the code. But he kept a wary eye on the clock. If Hannah thought he was going to allow her special favors, she'd better think again.

The resuscitation was winding down when suddenly Hannah spoke up from beside him. "Oh, look, it's noon. Guess I'd better get home. Have a great day," she said with obviously forced cheerfulness before turning and walking toward the trauma residents' call rooms.

Her biting sarcasm, for some odd reason, made him smile.

He shook his head, his previous frustration draining away. Hannah was a feisty one, no doubt about it. And until this moment he'd never considered feistiness to be an admirable trait in a woman.

Allie had pretty much agreed with whatever he'd said, twisting her personality into whatever she thought he wanted. And now he could admit he'd found her ready agreement very annoying.

Truthfully, there was far too much to admire about Hannah. Her strength, her intelligence, her willingness to learn, her obvious empathy toward her patients and the way she stood up for herself.

The crux of his problem was that he liked her as a

person. Respected her as a surgical resident. Desired her as a woman.

Where in the hell would he find the strength to stay away from her?

Hannah fell asleep the moment she got home and ended up sleeping far too long, well into the evening, which only served to screw up her entire sleep schedule as she was then wide-awake for over half the night.

Thinking of Jake. Reliving the passionate night they'd spent together at his condo. And every interaction they'd had since then.

Her butt was seriously dragging the next morning and as far as she was concerned, it was all Jake's fault.

It was ironic to realize that by the time she managed to get her sleep cycle back on track, it would be her turn to be on first call again.

She'd known going into the program that all residents took call every fourth night. But she hadn't fully appreciated how the first-year residents ended up fielding most of the phone calls to the point that the more senior residents got far more sleep.

At least she had something to look forward to after her first year as a resident was over. Just three-hundred and fifty-eight days to go.

Since that thought was totally depressing, she quickly shoved it aside. There was no point in wishing away her life.

She'd take each day for the learning experience it offered.

Jake was once again the attending physician on duty for her Saturday-night call. She was proud of how she'd managed to keep him at a distance over the past few days since their disastrous kiss in her call room. Every interaction with him had been cool and impersonal.

But during rounds it was just the two of them, creating an intimacy she found hard to ignore. Thankfully, their trauma pagers went off the moment they finished, so they ran down to the ED together. Their patient was a guy in his early thirties, with the size and stature of a football player, who'd fallen down a flight of stairs. He was already intubated and unconscious as she began her trauma assessment.

Without warning, he suddenly woke up, extremities flailing wildly. He smacked Hannah in the back of her head with his arm. Caught off guard, she ended up sprawled on top of him. When she lifted her head, trying to get her feet under her, she gasped when his other fist came flying straight at her face.

"Look out!" Jake shouted, and miraculously he caught the guy's fist inches before it could connect. "Are you all right?" he asked harshly, as she stumbled out of harm's way.

Numbly, she nodded, even though the back of her head still throbbed painfully. For a moment their gazes locked and she thought she saw a flash of concern in Jake's green eyes before he turned his attention to the patient.

"Get locking restraints on this guy now!" he ordered. "And give him ten milligrams of Versed to calm him down."

Within five minutes the muscle-bound patient was once again lying peacefully on the gurney, almost as if nothing had happened. It would have been comical if her head didn't hurt.

"Are you really all right?" Jake asked in an under-tone, after the patient had been to the CT scanner and back.

"I'm fine. Thanks for saving me from a broken nose."

Her lighthearted attempt at humor fell flat and for a moment it looked as if he wanted to say something more, but they were interrupted by the neurosurgeon coming into the trauma bay.

Leaving Jake to discuss the muscleman's head bleed, which they'd found on a CT scan, she retreated to the cafeteria to review her notes. No way did she want to make another careless mistake, the way she had with the dose of Mr. Turkow's antibiotics.

But images of Jake's concern kept flashing in her mind. After a quick meal she went to find ibuprofen for her headache.

The calls were sporadic, nothing serious. Until she was called up to the general floor because a patient needed IV antibiotics and the nurse wasn't able to get one in place.

Hannah went to the patient's bedside and introduced herself again. Mrs. Eva Carmichael was an elderly patient who'd had her gallbladder removed earlier that day by Dr. Holt, and just one glance at the woman's bruised arms convinced Hannah her veins were pretty much nonexistent.

"She's probably going to need a jugular or subclavian central line," Josie, the nurse, informed her in a low voice.

Hannah sighed. Jake had left pretty clear instructions during rounds about this particular patient. Any issues whatsoever were to go directly to him. Apparently

Mrs. Carmichael was a friend of Gregory Matthews's mother.

Nothing like having connections to the chief of surgery.

When Jake answered her page, she explained the situation.

"I'll be right up."

She hung up the phone and went back to Mrs. Carmichael's bedside. "Dr. Holt is going to come up to explain your options," she informed her.

"Thank you, dear," the elderly woman said kindly, patting her hand as if the patient-doctor roles were reversed. "He's such a nice young man, isn't he?"

Hannah's smile was strained. "Yes, he is. Very nice."

"And so handsome, too!" Mrs. Carmichael's eyes held a mischievous glint. "Don't you agree?"

"Yes, he's very handsome," she agreed again, trying to think of a way to change the subject.

"Hello," Jake greeted them both as he walked into the room. Hannah feared her expression gave her away when he shot a curious glance in her direction before going over to take the patient's hand. "How are you feeling, Mrs. C.?"

"A little achy, that's all," she responded. "We were just talking about you, Dr. Holt."

"Really? Good or bad?" he asked jokingly.

"Good, of course," Mrs. Carmichael said with a weak laugh that turned into a moan as she put her hand over the dressing covering her fresh surgical incision. "Hannah and I both think you're nice and handsome."

Hannah hoped he didn't notice her flush of embarrassment as she tried to get the conversation back on track. "Mrs. Carmichael's peripheral IV infiltrated just before her next dose of antibiotics was due. Rather than keep poking at her, I thought we should consider a central line."

"Hmm." Jake did a quick examination of the woman's arms and then nodded reluctantly. "Mrs. C., you understand that we need you to get a full course of antibiotics, as your gall bladder was infected. I think Dr. Stewart's assessment is right on. We really need to put a catheter into one of your large veins, either along your neck or beneath your clavicle." He indicated the areas he meant on her skin. "And what that means is that we'll have to do a minor surgical procedure."

"Are you going to put me to sleep?" she asked.

"No, ma'am," Hannah piped up. "But Dr. Holt is going to give you numbing medicine so it shouldn't hurt much. We will have to move you to the ICU for the procedure, but you'll come back here to your regular room when it's over. Shouldn't take more than an hour."

A loud beeping echoed in the room as their pagers went off. Hannah read the trauma alert—two motor-vehicle-crash victims from a head-on collision were on their way in.

"Actually, Dr. Stewart is going to put this catheter in for you," Jake corrected as he put his pager back in its holder. "But she's a great doctor, Mrs. C., so I'm leaving you in good hands."

Hannah's stomach clenched with dread, but she knew better than to say anything in front of the patient. Especially a VIP. "I'll make the arrangements," she said, and then quickly followed Jake out of the room.

"Meet me down in the trauma room when you're finished," he said as he headed for the stairwell.

"Wait a minute," she said, reaching out to grab his arm. "You can't seriously expect me to do this alone?"

"You've placed central lines before—in fact, we just did one the other day, didn't we?" he asked. But then he frowned, a flash of uncertainty in his gaze. "Unless your head hurts too much?"

As an excuse it would have been the easy way out, but, while tempted, she just couldn't do it. "No, my head is fine. But, Jake, she's a VIP!" Hannah couldn't believe he meant her to do the procedure all alone. What if something bad happened?

"Look, Hannah, I have two seriously injured patients on the way in, and Mrs. Carmichael's antibiotics are already overdue," Jake pointed out in a reasonable tone. "You're capable of putting the catheter in yourself. Get the medical student to assist, as Richard will be with me."

"But—"

"Don't forget to come down to the trauma bay as soon as you're finished," he said again, before heading down the stairs.

Helplessly, she watched him leave, wishing she dared put off the procedure until Jake could be there.

But what if they had a busy night? More trauma patients could arrive. If Mrs. Carmichael didn't get her antibiotics, she could go into septic shock. Besides, Hannah didn't want to have to explain to the chief why she hadn't got the line in.

She took a deep breath and let it out slowly. She could do this. She was a surgeon. And as Jake had said, she'd just put a central line in another patient two days ago.

This procedure would be no different.

Except that Mrs. Carmichael happened to be the mother of a friend of the chief's.

Don't think about it, she warned herself as she strode back to the nurses' station. She made the arrangements with Josie to have Mrs. Carmichael transported to the ICU and then she paged the medical student, Renee Anderson, to assist.

The ICU was extremely busy, so there wasn't anyone available to help out. The nurse dashed into the room long enough to put the patient on the heart monitor and to place the call light on the floor. "Step on this if you run into trouble," she advised, before dashing out again.

Hannah glanced curiously at Renee, who shrugged. "It works," the medical student said wryly. "Hey, it's easy enough to step on it while maintaining a sterile field."

Okay, then. Hannah explained the steps of the procedure to Mrs. Carmichael while Renee opened the sterile tray. Hannah donned her sterile garb, and then began to prep the site. Poor Mrs. Carmichael flinched a bit when she injected the Lidocaine. "I'm sorry, this is going to burn a little," Hannah apologized.

"I'm okay," the elderly lady said, her voice muffled beneath the sterile drapes.

Mrs. C. was a real trouper. If she was frightened in any way, she certainly didn't show it.

For some reason, the patient's confidence in her abilities helped Hannah relax.

She picked up the large-bore needle and then gestured for Renee to bring over the ultrasound machine. "I need you to help me find the subclavian vein," she instructed. "Draw the probe slowly across the skin."

Renee was also dressed in sterile garb and she took out a clean ultrasound probe and gently moved it over the area Hannah indicated, right beneath the clavicle bone.

"Stop. You have it right there," Hannah said when the vein lit up on the screen. She double-checked her landmarks with her thumb and middle finger. "Okay, Mrs. Carmichael, I'm going to insert the needle. Let me know if you feel any pain."

She slid the needle through the skin, grateful that the area was well numbed as the patient didn't move. She advanced the needle and then stopped the moment she hit a blood return. Holding the needle steady, she picked up the guide wire and threaded it through the end of the needle, slipping it farther into the blood vessel. Once the wire was in, the rest of the procedure went much easier.

"Are you okay under there?" Hannah asked, as she threaded the catheter over the guide wire.

"Yes, dear," Mrs. Carmichael responded faintly.

Suddenly the cardiac-monitor alarm began to beep, in a triple beep pattern that signaled the most urgent alarm.

"What's wrong?" Renee asked.

"V-tach," Hannah murmured in a grim voice, her heart lodging in her throat when she stared at the monitor. She knew there was always a risk of central venous catheters going in too far, tickling the heart muscle and causing arrhythmias, but the phenomenon had never happened to her.

"What should we do?" Renee asked, her voice rising in panic. "Step on the call light? Ask the nurse to call a code?"

"No, just give me a minute." Hannah hoped and prayed she was making the right decision as she fixed her gaze on the heart monitor and slowly pulled back on the guide wire.

CHAPTER SIX

"WHAT'S going on in here?" the nurse who'd put the call light on the floor demanded as she came running into the room.

"Everything is fine," Hannah said, sending the nurse a pointed glare. Didn't she realize the patient could hear every word they were saying? Even if there was a reason to panic, they didn't need to add to the patient's distress. But the emergency was short-lived. The cardiac monitor stopped beeping as Mrs. Carmichael's heart returned to a normal rhythm. The tension in the room evaporated.

"Are you okay, Mrs. Carmichael?" Hannah asked, feeling as if her own heart was in V-tach the way her pulse jumped erratically in her chest.

"I'm fine," the elderly woman murmured.

"I'm glad to hear that. The wire tickled your heart a little, causing the monitor to alarm, but everything is fine now. The catheter is in place—we just need to place a couple of stitches to keep it there."

"Whatever you say, dear," Mrs. Carmichael said, remaining amazingly calm.

Hannah took a deep breath, trying to control her jagged nerves. Thank heavens Mrs. Carmichael's condition had stabilized. She couldn't imagine how Jake would have reacted if she'd caused his VIP patient to code.

And she really didn't want to explain that to the chief of trauma surgery.

Good thing Mrs. Carmichael was so nice or this entire event could have been made out to look much worse.

Hannah finished stitching Mrs. Carmichael's catheter in place and then covered the area with a sterile, transparent dressing. She ordered a portable chest X-ray to verify proper placement and to rule out any potential complications, like a pneumothorax. After she confirmed everything was fine on the X-ray, she made arrangements for the elderly woman to return to her room, feeling strangely exhilarated.

She'd handled the potentially emergent situation pretty well all things considered. And she wanted someone to share the good news with.

Jake. She found herself wishing she could talk to Jake.

The knowledge was disturbing. Jake wasn't her friend or her confidant. And certainly not her lover.

He was her boss and, as such, he'd expect her to handle any emergency situation. Especially one that might have potentially been her fault. It could be that Mrs. Carmichael's potassium levels were out of whack or she'd put the guide wire in too far. Or both, she silently acknowledged.

After a brief discussion with the pharmacist about getting Mrs. Carmichael's antibiotics back on schedule, she headed down to the trauma room.

Halfway down the stairs, her cell phone chirped from the depths of her lab-coat pocket. She pulled it out and glanced at the text message, wondering who on earth would be contacting her. Her mother was usually the only one who called and her mother didn't have a clue how to text.

Hey, sis, out on parole. Call me.

She stopped abruptly, grabbing the rail so her momentum didn't cause her to fall flat on her face.

Dear God. Her brother Tristan was out of jail.

Hannah stared at the text message for a full minute, assailed by a wave of hope, almost overwhelmed by despair.

After a brief internal debate she thrust her phone back in her pocket without calling or responding to his text message. There wasn't time to get into a long conversation with her brother. Jake was waiting for her down in the trauma bay and the two motor-vehicle-crash patients deserved to take priority at the moment.

Besides, it wasn't likely her brother was calling to share good news. If she knew Tristan, he probably needed money. After all, being in debt was how he'd gotten in trouble in the first place.

And that was a situation she just couldn't deal with right now.

Jake glanced up, sensing the moment Hannah walked into the trauma bay, and frowned when he noted the strained expression on her face. Had he been wrong to trust her with Mrs. C.'s line placement? For a moment he feared the worst. "Problems with the procedure?"

"The guide wire tickled her heart, causing a few arrhythmias, but she's fine. The line is in good position and her antibiotics are infusing now."

For a moment he searched her gaze, realizing that,

despite the complication, she was proud of her accomplishment. "She does have a small frame, so you likely went in a little too far."

"Agreed. Luckily she bounced back quickly, tolerating the procedure really well."

He nodded, reluctantly impressed by the way she took responsibility for what had happened, rather than blaming something else. And a little V-tach during a line placement was fairly common. But if the procedure went well, what was bothering her? Did she still have a headache after getting whacked by their head-injured patient?

And why did he care if she had a headache or not? Wild, rambunctious patients were not uncommon on Trauma. She was lucky she hadn't suffered anything worse than a headache. One of his colleagues back in Minneapolis had suffered a broken jaw after being slugged by a patient.

Those moments when Hannah had been lying half-stunned over their patient, her face in the line of fire from the guy's fist, kept replaying over and over in his mind. Forcing him to acknowledge how he was failing miserably in his goal of keeping their relationship from becoming personal.

Granted, he would have reacted the same way if anyone else on his team had been in danger. But he doubted he'd continue dwelling on the event hours later.

He shouldn't be feeling so protective of her.

She walked over to the most recent trauma patient, as if intending to get caught up on the events that had transpired in her absence. Once again, she seemed determined to learn everything possible.

He couldn't remember any other first-year resident being this intense. And he couldn't help being curious as to why she'd chosen to be a surgeon in the first place. Other areas of medicine were far easier to manage.

But he sensed Hannah didn't take the easy way out, ever.

For the tenth time he found himself wishing Hannah had been in some other residency program, rather than here at Chicago Care. Because he'd never experienced a physical connection this strong with anyone else.

Certainly not with Allie. At least, he'd thought he had with Allie, only to discover the feelings had been all on his side, not hers.

"Did you see his labs?" Hannah asked, dragging his attention to the present.

The lab screen was directly in front of him, so he quickly scanned the results. "His lactic-acid level is high, likely due to necrotic bowel." Exactly as he'd suspected. "Call the O.R. and let them know we're coming up."

"Will do." He was surprised she didn't immediately ask if she could scrub in on the case.

Then again, none of his interactions with Hannah went the way he expected.

And why was that fact so intriguing?

As they headed to the O.R., Hannah's cell phone rang from the depths of her lab coat. He watched her punch a button, sending the call to voice mail.

Strange, as the time was well after midnight. Who on earth would be calling her?

A flash of jealousy caught him off guard, before he quickly reined it in. Hannah's personal life wasn't any of his business. They were nothing more than colleagues, and the sooner his brain figured that out, the better off he'd be.

Yet as they scrubbed in at the sinks in the core of the O.R., he could tell she was still upset, seemingly completely lost in her thoughts.

"You're not supposed to scrub so hard you draw blood," he murmured dryly.

She glanced up at him in surprise, and then dropped her gaze back down to her reddened hands.

"Sorry," she muttered, tossing aside the brush and then doing the final rinse.

He finished his rinse, as well. "You need to make sure your mind is focused when you enter the O.R.," he advised, trying to pretend he wasn't dying to know what was bothering her. "So put whatever issues you have aside until later, understand?"

"Got it," she said with a curt nod.

He wanted to say more, but heading into a surgical case wasn't the time or the place. As they began the procedure, he couldn't complain about the way she handled herself in the O.R. She seemed completely engrossed in the case at hand. He ended up taking a little extra time, allowing her to do a good portion of the procedure herself.

Not that he was giving her any special treatment or anything. He'd do the same for any of his residents.

A wide smile blossomed on her face when they'd stripped off their gloves and their masks when the case was finished, forcing him to acknowledge once again how different she was from any other resident. "That was awesome!" she exclaimed. "Thanks for letting me do so much."

"You're welcome," he muttered, knowing he was

sinking deeper under her spell every minute they spent together. Man, he needed to get a grip. He turned away, intending to put distance between them. "See you later. I need to head up to the ICU to check on the second trauma patient Richard is caring for."

"I'll come with you," she volunteered, catching up with him.

He stifled a low groan and tried not to look at her as they rode the elevator up to the third floor, but it wasn't easy. When her cell phone chirped again, he glanced at her, letting a hint of his exasperation show. "Do you want to talk about it?"

"What? The bowel resection?"

He wasn't fooled by her wide-eyed, innocent expression. She knew very well what he'd meant. "About whatever is bothering you. Every time that phone of yours goes off, you practically jump out of your skin."

"It's nothing," she said quickly. "Just some personal family stuff."

He shouldn't have been relieved by her answer, but he was. At least the persistent caller wasn't some former boyfriend or something. Still, her reluctance to talk inexplicably bothered him. When they reached the ICU, he paused outside the doors. "Take a break, Hannah. Deal with your family issues and then get your head back into patient care."

"My head is fully engaged with patient care," she replied stubbornly. "The personal stuff can wait."

It was on the tip of his tongue to argue, but in the end he let it go.

Reminding himself that whatever Hannah's problems were, they certainly weren't any of his business.

* * *

Hannah did her best to focus on the conversation between Richard and Jake regarding their female trauma patient, Isabella Cronin, who'd suffered multiple pelvic fractures after crashing into a tree.

Yet her mind kept drifting back to Jake's unexpected offer to talk about her personal problems.

Surprisingly, she'd been sorely tempted to unload her messed-up family situation on him, even though she knew that was the worst thing she could do. The shame of growing up in the Chicago projects was something she couldn't shed like a second skin.

Especially considering her mother, disabled by severe rheumatoid arthritis, still lived in the low-income, city-subsidized housing. Just five years ago, her mother's condition had gotten so bad she hadn't been able to continue her job as a waitress in a diner, so Hannah had started supporting her financially.

And now she'd probably end up supporting her brother, too.

If Jake knew anything about her background, or the truth about some of the things she'd done, he'd look at her differently, and the last thing she wanted was for him to begin judging her performance on something other than her abilities as a surgeon.

The very thought of being treated differently nearly made her break out into a cold sweat. She'd kept her past, and the mistakes she'd made, well hidden for too long to let the secret out now.

"Make sure she remains NPO for possible surgery tomorrow morning," Jake advised.

She dragged her attention to the patient before them. "Shouldn't we start her on heparin, as she'll be lying in bed for an extended period of time?"

Richard gave an exasperated sigh and she immediately realized she'd missed something important.

"We can't give any anticoagulation to patients with a head injury," Jake said mildly. "And her CT scan showed a questionable area that could be a small subdural hematoma."

"I see," she murmured, wishing she'd kept her stupid mouth shut. Her own fault, for obsessing about her personal problems.

No more lapses in concentration, she told herself sternly. As Jake had pointed out the other day, inattention to detail could kill a patient.

"Any other questions?" Jake asked.

"Nope." Thankfully, her pager went off again. "Excuse me," she said, moving away to find a phone.

The floor nurse on the other end of the line was clearly upset. "This guy's going crazy! We need you here, *now*!"

She dropped the phone and ran.

The patient's room was complete chaos when she arrived. The patient was a forty-year-old man who'd come in with a ruptured appendix. He was shouting obscenities and had tossed his bedside table and his dinner tray across his room.

"Get Security in here," she ordered, suspecting that talking him down was out of the question. He was post-op day three and she suspected he might be having DTs from alcohol withdrawal. Grimly, she realized she should have given him something to sedate him earlier. "We need this guy placed in restraints."

Four security officers arrived and assisted in wrestling the guy down, as the nurses were afraid to get anywhere near him, not that she could blame them. She knew, only too well, what it felt like to be slugged by a patient.

Her pager went off with yet another trauma call. She stifled a sigh. At the rate this night was going, she wouldn't even get one hour of sleep.

It wasn't until they'd gotten the rambunctious patient safely placed in four-point locking restraints that she bothered to scroll through her page. Two victims with multiple gunshot wounds. Great. Just what she needed.

"Give him two milligrams of Ativan, and if that doesn't work to keep him calm, you can repeat it times one. I'll be back to check on him later."

"I'm sorry, you have to write that order before you leave," the nurse said.

She tamped down her temper, knowing the nurse was only following the rules. Rules that had sounded logical enough during orientation but that seemed ridiculous at times like this. Grabbing the chart, she wrote the order very neatly, to prevent any errors, despite being in a hurry. Afterward she bolted down to the trauma room, taking the stairs two at a time.

There were at least a dozen people filling the room, mostly police officers. She could barely see the patients. "What happened?" she asked when Jake waved her over.

"Two young men were caught robbing a liquor store. They tried to shoot at the cops and earned multiple gunshot wounds as a result. This guy has a gunshot wound to the chest—I'm waiting for the cardiothoracic surgeons. You'd better take that one there—he's not as badly off. His gunshot wounds are in his extremities, one in his arm and the other in his leg."

"Okay." Hannah walked over to her patient and sucked in a harsh breath when she saw him. Tristan? No, it couldn't be. She leaned over, trying to see past the blood. Same facial features and brown hair, but not Tristan. Thank God. Looking at him more closely confirmed the patient was probably a year or two younger than Tristan.

As she began cleaning out the gunshot wounds to investigate the extent of the damage, she did her best to ignore the sick feeling clenching her stomach. This kid wasn't Tristan, but it just as easily could have been. If not Tristan, one of his not-too-bright friends.

Coming face-to-face with the past she'd tried to leave behind wasn't easy. Especially since Tristan had just gotten out of jail where he'd served the past three years for armed robbery.

CHAPTER SEVEN

HANNAH did her best to remain objective as she cared for the young gunshot victim, but it wasn't easy. All the conflicted feelings she had toward Tristan crowded her brain. She pushed them aside, as best she could, to focus on her patient.

How he'd been injured wasn't her issue. She had to be concerned with repairing the damage, regardless of the cause.

Her victim's name was Devon Wallace, and his arm wound wasn't too bad as the bullet had gone through cleanly. Some muscle damage, sure, but nothing serious.

The leg wound was another matter. He had a significant amount of bleeding from his thigh, despite the pressure dressing that had been placed by the paramedics to minimize blood loss. In addition, there was no exit wound, from what she could tell. She had a sinking suspicion that the bullet was lodged near or partially inside the artery.

The policemen hovered right behind her, practically looking over her shoulder, making it clear to the hospital staff that the two victims she and Jake were working on were their prisoners as well as patients. Their presence was rather intimidating, to say the least.

"Get me a vascular surgical tray," Hannah said to the nurse. "I need to explore Devon's bullet wound and possibly repair the damage."

"Doctor, we need the bullet as evidence once you're able to remove it," the officer closest to her said. He was a young man, close to her own age, but the bleak expression in his eyes betrayed how he'd seen too much ugliness in his line of work.

A fact she could, unfortunately, relate to. She gave a curt nod, to show she understood his request.

During her early teenage years, cops had been an authority figure she'd been taught to avoid at all costs. But since entering medical school, she'd been forced to reassess her opinion. From the very beginning, she'd learned that cops and health-care workers had a strange sort of bond between them. Maybe because they were both public servants.

Cops were there to protect and the doctors and nurses were there to heal.

"Believe me, once I get the bleeding under control, it's all yours," she said.

"Here's the vascular tray, Dr. Stewart," the nurse announced as she placed the covered tray on the bedside table. The young officer stepped back to give her room to work. As Hannah pulled on sterile gloves, the nurse unwrapped the sterile covering over the instruments.

"Give him five milligrams of morphine and five milligrams of Versed," she ordered. "And then help me remove the pressure dressing."

Even though she'd given him enough sedation to knock him out, she still picked up the prefilled needle and syringe and injected Lidocaine into the edges of the wound to numb the area. The last thing she needed was for Devon to jerk away and cause more damage to the artery. Luckily, the drug combination worked, as he didn't flinch when she made the first incision. There was a lot of blood coming from the wound as she used the scalpel to widen the entry wound to expose the length of the artery, the better to gauge the injury.

After mopping up more blood, she glanced at the nurse. "Give him two units of O-negative blood," Hannah ordered. "And get him type and crossmatched for more."

Jake came up beside her, and instantly her senses went on alert, in a very different way than when the young, good-looking cop had done the same thing. Why, oh, *why* did Jake have this affect on her? "Are you okay?" he asked in a low voice, as if they were the only two people in the trauma bay.

She nodded, determined to ignore her reaction to him. "Yes, but I'll need your help if the artery has been nicked. There's a lot of blood, indicating the artery has likely been damaged."

"The CT surgeon is here to evaluate Joey, the kid with the gunshot wound to the chest, so I'll be free to help in a few minutes," he promised. "I'll arrange for an O.R. team to be on stand by, in case we need to do a full graft replacement."

"Sounds good," she murmured. Jake moved away, and while she should have been relieved, she missed the security of having him close by as she continued to work on Devon's wound. Exploring farther, she eventually found the bullet, lodged right near the femoral artery.

From what she could tell, there was also a very slight tear in the artery.

Not too badly damaged. She was hopeful they could do the repair here in the ED.

Whether he realized it or not, Devon was extremely lucky the cop hadn't shot a millimeter to the left, or he would probably have lost his leg or bled to death before getting to the hospital. Even with the pressure dressing the paramedics had applied, and the tiny tear, he'd lost a lot of blood.

She'd certainly seen patients die from a femoral-artery injury. A bit ironic seeing as he'd survive long enough to serve his jail time.

Using the clamps from the tray, she did her best to isolate the area of the tear and then worked on removing the bullet. "Nurse, grab a specimen cup for the evidence," she instructed.

The nurse opened up a sterile container and then stood waiting. Hannah gently grasped the bullet with the pickups and slowly drew it out of the wound. She dropped the mashed bullet inside.

The nurse closed it and then turned to hand the evidence over to the cop. He took it and then pulled out a slip of paper and a pen.

"I need both of your full names to verify the chain of evidence," he said, with a hint of apology in his tone. "In case we need you to testify in court."

Great, just what she needed. Would they look into her background, as well? She certainly hoped not. The nurse gave her name and then the officer glanced at her.

"Hannah Joy Stewart," she said curtly, hoping he wasn't serious about the possibility of testifying.

"Could I have your address, too?" he asked. "In case we need to send a subpoena?"

"Give him the hospital address," Jake advised, coming up beside her, pulling on a sterile gown and gloves. "Since this is work related, he doesn't need your personal address."

"Trust me, I could get her personal address if I wanted to," the officer said dryly.

There was a tense moment as the two men stared at each other, giving Hannah the distinct impression they saw her as some sort of chew-toy to fight over. It might have been funny if Devon's artery hadn't been clamped for almost two minutes.

Jake looked away first, turning his attention to Devon's wound. She moved aside to give him room to work. Since the officer was still waiting, she went ahead and gave him her home address, figuring the cop was right—no doubt he could find out where she lived if he really wanted to.

And the last thing she wanted was for a cop, any cop, to start probing into her background. What if he found out about Tristan? The very idea made her stomach clench painfully.

"Thanks, Dr. Stewart," he said, with a satisfied smile.

She nodded again, and then leaned over to watch what Jake was doing. He had the artery repaired in less than a minute.

"Release the clamp, slowly," he instructed.

She did as he asked, releasing the clamp slowly so they could be sure the sutures at the repair site would hold. When there was no more blood loss, she breathed a tiny sigh of relief.

Now for the real test, full circulation. "Check for pulses in his feet," she said to the nurse. There was a moment of silence as the nurse palpated the top of Devon's foot and then slowly nodded.

"I feel a pulse. It's weak, but it's there."

"Excellent," Jake murmured. "Good save." Why she clung pathetically to every ounce of praise he doled out, she had no clue. He stepped aside and gestured to the wound. "Because of the contamination from the bullet, you'll need to irrigate the wound very well before you close."

She glanced up at him in surprise. He was going to allow her to close the entire wound, muscle and all? Not that she was planning to argue. Thrilled with the chance, she nodded. "Understood."

After only placing a couple of sutures, she was interrupted when the doors from the ambulance bay burst open and two women rushed in.

"Devon! Joey!" the older of the two women shouted. For being older, she moved fast, reaching Hannah and grabbing her arm before the cops surged forward.

"Get back!" the officer yelled, dragging the woman away from Hannah and the sterile field. "Get out of here. No visitors allowed!"

"You can't keep me from my sons!" the woman screeched, fighting against the cops who were physically pushing her out of the way, back outside the trauma bay. "I'll call a lawyer!"

"Go ahead—your sons are going to need a lawyer," the cop responded grimly, "as they're both prisoners in our custody. They're under arrest for armed robbery and attempting to shoot a police officer, which means no visitors!"

Hannah tried to shut out the commotion, even though her heart was racing at the unexpected interruption. She knew only too well how prisoner patients didn't get the same privileges as other patients because they were essentially in custody.

Jake glanced at her, silently asking if she was okay.

She wasn't, but he didn't know, couldn't know, how this entire scenario hit too close to home.

As she finished closing Devon's wound, she knew the woman who'd rushed into the emergency department could have been her mother trying to see her brother. Or, for that matter, she might have been the one trying to bulldoze her way into seeing her brother.

Because, no matter how badly Tristan had screwed up his life, she still loved him.

Jake went to find Hannah, once he'd assured himself that the two gunshot victims were settled in their respective beds. Joey was in the ICU after getting the bullet removed from his chest, and Devon was up on the general surgical floor.

She'd handled the femoral artery injury very well, despite her nervousness. Not that she let much of her inner turmoil show, except for near the end, when the mother of the victim had rushed in.

Hannah had looked as if she'd wanted to let the patient's mother see her son, not that he could blame her. But the cop had stood by his rules of prisoner patients having no visitors.

He wanted to talk to Hannah, to make sure she was really doing okay, but he also had to find Richard. Twice tonight he'd needed Richard's assistance only he hadn't been there for him.

He needed to have a chat with Richard, and soon. Just because the attending physicians were now required to take call, it was no reason for the senior residents to slack off on their responsibilities.

Jake hesitated, knowing he should put work concerns first, but he couldn't do it. Instead, he went to find Hannah.

When he walked onto the general-surgery floor, he frowned when he found her standing in the hallway outside Devon's room, talking to the young officer that had been down in the trauma bay. The way they were talking in low, hushed voices grated on his nerves. What was she thinking, flirting with a cop?

The walls around his heart hardened. So much for thinking he had a certain connection with Hannah. Was he falling into the same trap as he had with Allie?

The possibility was terrifying.

"Dr. Stewart, do you have a minute to discuss patient care?" he asked in a hard, sarcastic tone.

She looked surprised to see him, but the cop didn't. The cop glared at him, as if annoyed at the interruption. But Hannah seemed oblivious to the tension between them. "Of course. I'll see you later, Sam."

Sam? Sam? They were on a first-name basis? What the hell was she thinking? And why did he care?

"Flirt on your own time, not mine," he snapped when he headed toward the ICU at such a brisk pace she needed to jog to catch up.

"Flirt? What are you talking about?" she demanded.

"You heard me. It's obvious to me and every other person in the hospital that the cop wants to date you, a fact I couldn't care less about except that we happen to have a critically ill patient who requires your attention."

Hannah's mouth dropped open in shock at his accusation. The moment the words left his mouth, he wondered if he'd crossed the line. Yet he couldn't seem to stop.

"Don't act so surprised," he continued in the same sarcastic tone. "You're too smart to be that clueless."

"You're crazy," she sputtered. "He's a nice guy, that's all. I was trying to understand his no-visitor rule. I'm not interested in dating anyone. But if I were, the *last* person I'd choose is a cop."

The frankness of her tone made him think she might be telling the truth. And he just barely caught himself before he could ask why a cop might be the last person she'd choose to go out with.

He leveled his tone with an effort. "Who you date isn't my business, but Joey is. His condition is critical. I need you to keep a close eye on him for the rest of the night." Jake tried to pretend the cozy chat between Hannah and the cop hadn't made him see red. "Joey's blood pressure is low, yet he can't get too much volume through blood products because the CT surgeons had to repair the hole in his heart. You'll need to walk a very fine line with him."

"Understood." Her annoyance couldn't have been any clearer if she'd displayed it across a billboard. Had he misjudged the coziness between them? And what difference did it make one way or the other? "What would you like me to do if his blood pressure drops? Start vasopressors? Or give him more volume?"

After he finished explaining how he wanted Joey's care managed, he turned and left the ICU, feeling like a fool.

He scrubbed a hand over his face. Why had he over-reacted to seeing her talking with the young, handsome cop who had made it clear he wouldn't have minded asking her out? It wasn't as if he had any claim on Hannah. If she and the cop hit it off, great. Why did he care?

He needed to stop comparing everything she did to Allie. It was his own fault that he'd fallen for Allie, never once considering he'd been nothing more than a shiny prize she'd wanted to win.

So far, Hannah wasn't tripping over herself to get his attention. She wasn't flirting with him as if he were the greatest thing in the world.

Most of all, Hannah hadn't gone into medicine for the selfish reasons Allie had become a nurse, to snag a rich doctor for a husband. The memory of listening to Allie laugh about it with her best friend still made him burn with humiliation.

Mentally kicking himself for allowing his emotions to get tangled over Hannah, he headed down to his call room. He threw himself onto the bed and closed his eyes but, no matter how much he tried to rest, he couldn't sleep. Every interaction he had with Hannah seemed to mock him.

After about an hour he gave up, deciding instead to head back up to the ICU. Joey's case was complicated and, truthfully, Richard should be handling his care, not an intern.

He told himself he wasn't going there to see Hannah. Or to apologize for his behavior. Although maybe he should, if the opportunity presented itself.

No. He was going to keep his distance. She could date whoever the hell she wanted. In fact, if she did find someone else, maybe he'd be able to move on with his life.

But not the cop. Or any of the other residents in the program. Or any of the other attending physicians on staff. Or anyone at all in the entire hospital.

Losing it. He was seriously losing it.

Disgusted with himself, he walked down the hall from the elevator toward the ICU and came across Hannah standing in the hallway, talking in a low voice on her cell phone. Ridiculous to be relieved she wasn't out talking to the cop.

He knew he should back off to give her privacy, but despite her low tone he couldn't help overhearing part of the conversation.

"I'm sorry, Mom, but I can't talk to you now. I have a sick patient in the ICU."

Her mother was calling at five-thirty in the morning? Had to be some sort of emergency. He couldn't help thinking that she never should have ignored those earlier calls. In an effort to make up for the way he'd treated her, Jake stepped forward, capturing Hannah's gaze. "It's okay," he whispered. "I'll take over on Joey for now. Go ahead and take the call."

Hannah frowned and shook her head, vehemently. Clearly she didn't want to talk to her mother. She turned away and hunched her shoulders. "No, Mom, I don't have more money to send. I'm sorry, but I can't earn more money by working extra hours—this job takes every bit of spare time I have. I don't know how we'll deal with the added expense of Tristan being home. He's an adult, he could try to help."

There was another pause and then she said, "No way,

I don't have time to talk to Tristan now. I'm busy. I'll talk to him later," then she hung up.

Jake couldn't pretend he hadn't overheard, especially when he was bothered by the tone of the call. Was it possible Hannah's mother was having some sort of financial crisis? It would be rough for Hannah to try and help out on a measly intern's salary. When she turned back toward him, the bleak expression in her eyes tugged at a heart he'd thought immune to emotion.

"Hannah, are you all right?"

"Yes." But her response was clipped and she avoided his gaze in a way that suggested she was anything but all right. "The general surgical unit just paged me to let me know that Devon is running a fever. Do you think we need to add another antibiotic?"

"Not yet. It's not exactly surprising he's running a fever, considering he was shot twice," Jake explained. "Give the antibiotics you've ordered a chance to work. If he's still running fever after twenty-four hours, we'll consider changing the medication to provide broader coverage."

"Fine."

When she moved to walk away, he stopped her with a hand on her arm. "Hannah, wait. Is there something you need? Something I can do for you? Is everything all right at home?"

The muscles of her arm stiffened beneath his fingers. "Look, Jake," she said finally, "you can't have it both ways. Either I'm flirting with the cop, or I'm not. Either we're working together as professionals, or we're not. You'll have to clue me in here as to what you want, because I can't figure it out. I'm tired and my head hurts."

She was right. He couldn't have it both ways. But staying away from her, keeping his distance from her, wasn't working so well. "We could be friends, Hannah," he offered. Her eyes widened in shock and he squelched a flash of annoyance. What was wrong with being friends? Surely the concept wasn't foreign to her. "And as a friend, I'm willing to listen, anytime you want to talk."

"I—uh—gosh—uh—that's very nice," she fumbled, looking more uncomfortable with the thought than when he'd had her naked in his bed. "But—ah—I really think I should try to get some sleep."

"A little late for that. It's five-thirty, and rounds begin in an hour," he pointed out.

But she was already backing away, and he knew she wasn't going to let him get close. "I know, don't worry, I'll be ready." And then she left, practically tripping over her own feet in her haste to get away from him.

He should be glad she was putting distance between them, but he wasn't. Instead, he had to fight the urge to go after her.

CHAPTER EIGHT

HANNAH didn't bother trying to sleep. Between her mother's phone call and Jake's offer to lend a friendly ear, she couldn't figure out what to do next.

Her mother's pleas for help kept reverberating in her head. And the old familiar guilt wouldn't leave her alone. But no matter how much she wanted to help her mother and her brother, the reality of being on call every fourth night made it clear that there was no way she could pick up a shift or two at Satin, even if she wanted to.

Which she really didn't.

She was still stunned by Jake's offer to be friends. Just thinking about it made her wince. The concept was nice, but the way her body responded when he was near was anything but friendly.

No, being friends wouldn't work.

An impossible situation.

Why did she seem to have such a strange connection to him? If he had been a lawyer or financial consultant, like she'd thought when she first met him down by the marina, would she still feel the same way?

Maybe. But if his career had been anything other than a doctor who happened to be on staff at Chicago Care, she doubted that she would have seen him again.

Granted, she would have thought about him, and probably would have wondered how he was doing, but that would have been the end of it.

She wouldn't have worked with him for hours on end. Or been given the chance to know him.

Impossible as it seemed, they'd grown closer over the week they'd worked together. The countless hours they'd spent together had caused them to understand each other better than if they'd gone out on traditional dates. Slowly, she was learning to like Jake the doctor as much as she'd been drawn to Jake the man.

The thought of letting Jake in on her family secrets made her stomach knot with anxiety. She'd tried to confide in Alec and that hadn't worked at all. Margie probably knew the most about her past, but even Margie didn't know everything.

No one did.

Suddenly her overwhelming exhaustion had nothing to do with being up all night and everything to do with the burden of shame she carried.

Would it be the worst thing in the world to share a tiny part of the burden with someone else? With someone she trusted?

With Jake?

Her turbulent thoughts kept her tossing and turning on the narrow cot in the call room until it was time to get up, shower and dress for morning rounds.

When she arrived on the unit, Jake looked a little rough around the edges, too. With a guilty start, she realized he'd been on call all week. Good grief, no wonder he looked exhausted.

"Good morning," she murmured.

"Good morning. Did you get any sleep?" he asked, as they waited for the rest of the team to show up.

"No. You?"

"No."

She stared at him and then laughed incredulously. "And here I was thinking that once I finished my year as an intern I'd get more sleep during my call shifts. Guess the joke is on me."

The corner of his mouth tipped up in a reluctant smile. "Yeah, but remember I'm generally only on call for one week every month and a half, you're on call every fourth day for the next five years. Big difference."

"Oh, good, that makes me feel so much better," she assured him, with a hint of playful sarcasm in her tone.

There was a strange expression in his eyes, giving her the impression he wanted to say something more, but then both Andrea and Richard walked up and the moment was gone.

Morning rounds were uneventful this time, no mistakes for Jake to point out to the group, thank heavens. And after they finished and she was relieved of her duties, she once again went back down to the trauma bay to observe for a while before heading home.

She wasn't surprised when Jake came up beside her. In fact, she'd secretly been waiting for him. "We have to stop meeting like this," he joked.

She let out a wry laugh. "Yeah, but I promise to leave by noon. I have no intention of jeopardizing your program."

"I know. That's not why I'm here." He was silent for a moment, then said, "You realize that avoiding your family isn't going to solve your problems, don't you?"

She slowly nodded, too tired to keep up the pretense. "Yeah, I know. But honestly? I don't have any more to give. Not emotional energy, time or money. Not without sacrificing my career. And knowing that makes me feel bad."

"Is there anything I can do to help?" Jake asked, his expression serious.

She was tempted, so tempted to ask for a hug, but they were standing in the back of the trauma bay with all of their colleagues around.

And hugging stretched the boundaries well beyond friendship.

Bad idea. She shouldn't be depending on Jake anyway. She shook her head. "Not really, but thanks for asking."

"Hannah, why don't we get out of here for a while?" he asked in a low voice. "We're both officially off duty. We could grab breakfast or lunch somewhere outside the hospital."

She glanced at the earnest expression in his eyes and felt her resistance melt away. He'd offered friendship, hadn't he? Just because she didn't have a lot of experience with having men as friends, it didn't mean she couldn't try, right? It wasn't as if she was going to date him.

No matter what, she couldn't afford to jeopardize her spot in the program by dating him.

"That actually sounds good. I'd love to get something to eat, but I hope you don't mind if we find someplace that serves breakfast food. For some reason, I can't face anything stronger than eggs and bacon after being up all night."

"I don't mind at all," he assured her. "I'm the same

way. Looks like the trauma resuscitation is winding down. Are you ready to go?"

Wryly she realized she'd completely missed all the key points of the resuscitation, so there was no point in staying. "Yes, I'm ready."

"Great. Should I meet you out in the parking structure?" he asked. "We can flip a coin to see who drives."

"No contest, considering I don't have a car," she was forced to confess. "I take the subway to work."

"Good, that makes things easier." The satisfaction in his tone was unmistakable. "I'll drive. There's a great restaurant a couple miles from here that serves breakfast all day."

She picked up her backpack off the floor, intending to sling it over her shoulder, but Jake intercepted it, shouldering her burden instead.

Leaving her no choice but to follow him outside, hoping and praying this impromptu breakfast wasn't a huge mistake.

Jake glanced at Hannah seated across from him at the local family restaurant, trying to convince himself this wasn't a date.

Surely he was capable of spending time with her, talking to her, as a friend.

So why did his gaze keep lingering on her face? Her brilliant blue eyes? Her long blond hair, curling enticingly around her face because she hadn't pulled it back into the usual braid after her morning shower?

And why was he tempted to drag her out of the noisy restaurant to take her somewhere quiet? Like his place?

Images of their night together slammed into his head, and he ruthlessly shoved them away. He tore his gaze from her to stare down at the menu—vowing to keep his insatiable desire for her under strict control.

After they gave their order, Hannah met his gaze over her mug of coffee. "So tell me, why do the attending physicians have to take in-hospital call?"

"It's just the trauma surgeons that have to take in-house call, not all attending physicians," he corrected. "And that's a new requirement that I implemented when I came."

"But why?" Hannah persisted.

"We took in-house call at the teaching hospital where I worked before and as much as we griped about it, we had the lowest mortality rates of any trauma center in the region. I was brought here to Chicago Care to turn this trauma program around so I instituted the same requirement, much to the dismay of my colleagues."

Hannah raised a brow. "I can imagine," she murmured.

He shrugged. "Yeah, but it's all about patient care, right? That's what counts in the end, how many lives we're able to save." He could have gone on about the other changes he planned to make for the trauma program, but surprisingly he was more interested in what was going on with Hannah's family. "Are you going to call your mother back?"

She dropped her gaze, staring blindly into her coffee mug. "Eventually," she allowed. "It's just that right now—it all seems so hopeless. There isn't anything more I can do."

"Surely she supports the demands of your career?"

He was trying not to be rude by asking outright what was going on.

Hannah surprised him by grimacing and lifting a shoulder. "Sort of."

What did that mean? "Maybe you need to explain it?"

She let out a weak laugh. "I have. She thinks I'm exaggerating to avoid helping her." She was silent for a moment, before meeting his gaze. "It's not all her fault. She has arthritis and can't work, so she does need financial support."

"I see," he murmured. Talk about a difficult situation. It was a little disturbing, the way he instinctively tuned into her emotions. "Is she okay at home by herself?"

"Yes. My aunt stops by every week to check on her, and she can get around on her own. But she resents me for not being around more."

"And your father?" he asked, hoping she wouldn't take offense.

She shrugged. "Took off when I was ten. We haven't seen him since."

"I'm sorry, Hannah." He reached across the table to take her hand. "I'm sure that must have been rough."

She didn't answer and he knew there was probably more to the story, but since she didn't offer any more information he told himself not to pry. "Hannah, you're going to be a great surgeon someday. Don't let yourself get sidetracked from obtaining your goal."

"I'm trying not to," she said in a voice barely above a whisper. "But what if obtaining my goal means turning my back on my family when they need me? Is that fair?"

He wasn't sure what to say to that, and a wave of

panic filled his chest at the thought of Hannah dropping out of the program.

A few days ago he would have been happy with that news. Hadn't he tried to convince her to transfer to another service? Now he knew he'd go to great lengths to keep her. "I'll help in any way I can."

"Thanks, but there isn't really anything you can do." She tugged on her hand and reluctantly he let go.

Seconds later the waitress arrived with their food, and Hannah seemed extremely interested in her veggie omelet while he dug into his steak and eggs.

"This is excellent," she murmured with a sigh. "I was hungrier than I realized."

He was hungry too, but not for food. Desperately, he steered the conversation to lighter matters, like the chances of the Chicago Cubs making it to the play-offs. But after they finished eating, and he'd paid the tab, at his insistence, they walked outside, where Hannah stopped and reached for her backpack, making it clear their friendly breakfast was over. "Thanks again, Jake. I'll take the subway home from here."

He couldn't help his visceral reaction. "No, you won't."

She looked surprised by his flat refusal. "There's no reason for you to go out of your way," she protested.

"You're not taking the subway." He couldn't seem to stop himself from feeling possessive. "Be reasonable. You've been up most of the night." She'd refused to let him take her home after the night they'd spent together too, and it had bothered him then the same way it bothered him now. "I'm driving you home and that's that."

For a moment she stared at him, and then gave in,

throwing her hands up in surrender. "Fine, if it's such a big deal, you can drive me home."

"About time you listen to reason," he said, trying not to sound irritable as he held the passenger door for her. Once he'd stored her backpack behind the driver's seat, he slid in and then glanced at her. "So? Which way?"

"North about five miles," she said shortly.

He followed her reluctant directions and ultimately stopped in front of a warehouse type of building that didn't look at all as if there were actual apartments inside.

For a moment he wondered if she was lying to him about living here, but before he could ask, she opened the passenger door and moved to get out. "Thanks for the ride," she said, avoiding his gaze.

"Wait." He lightly grasped her arm, unwilling to end things like this. "Hannah, please. Don't be upset. I'm sorry if I offended you."

"You didn't." Her snippy tone wasn't exactly reassuring.

When he simply raised a brow, she hunched her shoulders and rolled her eyes.

"Okay, maybe you did." Her expression softened to mild exasperation. "Has anyone ever told you how bossy you are?"

"As I'm a surgeon, that's not exactly a surprise," he said. "Yeah, I'm bossy. But you're stubborn."

"Independent," she corrected.

"Stubbornly independent," he said by way of compromise, although he kept hold of her arm. Dammit, he didn't want to let her go.

"Which is only going to make me a good surgeon," she pointed out reasonably.

He chuckled. "Okay, I'll give you that one." He glanced again at her unorthodox apartment building. "Does this apartment building of yours have any safety features for a woman living alone?"

"There's a lock with an intercom. What more do you want?" When he frowned, she let out a sigh. "Jake, it's very sweet of you to care, but I'm not used to anyone worrying about me," she admitted.

He knew she wasn't saying that to get sympathy but because it was the truth. Her dad was gone, her mother leaned on her for support. He imagined she was the one who'd held things together at home. The responsible one. But she didn't have to carry her burden alone. "You have friends now, people like me who are going to worry about you, so you may as well get used to it."

The skeptical expression on her face wasn't exactly reassuring. "Ah, okay. Did you want to come up for a minute? I can show you around."

His heart leaped with excitement, but he tried not to let his eagerness show. Going up with her wasn't exactly what a friend would do, but he couldn't walk away. Not now.

Not from Hannah. "Yes. I'd like that."

Hannah silently acknowledged that she was probably making a big mistake by letting Jake come up with her, but she couldn't seem to stop herself.

Yet she was somewhat surprised and disappointed when he didn't try to kiss her the moment the elevator doors closed.

"My parents are divorced," he offered, breaking the suddenly strained silence. "My dad and I, well, we don't exactly get along."

Logically, she knew Jake's situation was vastly different from hers, but she jumped on the slight similarity anyway. "Why not? I'm sure he's proud of your success."

Jake slowly shook his head. "No, he was sorely disappointed that I didn't follow in his footsteps by becoming a lawyer."

"Why does it matter? It's not as if being a surgeon isn't a noble career choice."

They reached her apartment door, and he stood close, almost too close as she used her key to unlock it. "Yeah, but he had visions of me being a partner in his firm. And because my mother was a physician's assistant, he saw my choice of becoming a doctor as a betrayal. Like I was siding with her or something."

His response disturbed her. "You're not a toy for them to fight over."

For a moment he stared at her. "I think that's the nicest thing anyone has ever said to me," he murmured. "Thank you."

The frank approval in his eyes made her feel lightheaded. And she realized she'd made a mistake in inviting him in.

"You're welcome," she managed, her voice barely above a whisper. Frantically, she tried to think of a way to get him to leave.

Suddenly, he moved closer, framed her face with his hands and then captured her mouth with a devastating kiss.

CHAPTER NINE

HER mind told her to resist, but her body responded to his passion with surprising urgency, flames of desire consuming all thought. She'd wanted this for what seemed like forever! His mouth was like a drug she constantly craved. When his tongue possessed hers, she allowed herself to be swept away in the heat of the moment, either because of her bone-weary fatigue or because of a simple lack of willpower when it came to his kisses.

Because his kisses were truly incredible.

This time he was the one tugging at their clothing, and his warm hands on her bare back made her gasp and press urgently against him.

The shrill ringing of her cell phone gave her pause and instantly the grim reality of her situation intruded, breaking through the veil of euphoria.

Her world was her mother living with arthritis in city-subsidized housing, and Tristan being out of jail on parole. Not an attending doctor who just happened to be in charge of the entire trauma-surgery program.

"We can't," she gasped, fighting for breath as she tore herself away to search blindly for her cell phone. Of course it was in the backpack lying on the floor at their feet. She pulled it out of the front pocket, her heart sinking when she realized the caller was once again Tristan. She dropped the phone back into the pocket, letting the call go to voice mail.

"Hannah, let me help you," Jake urged, breathing heavily, his eyes glittering with desire. "You don't have to face your family troubles alone."

She shook her head, taking several steps backward, putting badly needed distance between them. He had no clue just how far apart their worlds were. He didn't even realize she couldn't have afforded this warehouse apartment if not for Margie paying more than half the rent. "I'm sorry, but you were right. A personal relationship between us won't work."

For a moment Jake stared at her in shock, as if she'd accused him of something horrible. It was painful to watch him draw away from her. "I'm sorry," Jake said stiffly. "I shouldn't have crossed the line of friendship."

Friendship? She might have burst out laughing if every nerve in her body didn't long for him to pull her back into his arms to pick up where they'd just left off.

The kiss they'd shared had just proven how impossible it would be to try and remain friends. "Don't worry about it," she said lightly, as if her heart didn't feel bruised and battered from the loss. "I just think it would be best if I took your advice about not letting anything get in the way of reaching my goal of becoming a surgeon."

His gaze narrowed, and she sensed he wanted to argue, but he didn't. "Don't worry, I won't stand in your way. Although I could help, you know. I have a lot I could teach you."

Just the thought of trying to cash in on their friendship made her feel sick to her stomach. "I don't want your help, not like this. I want to be treated with the same respect as every other intern on your service."

There was another long pause, as she sensed he wanted to argue. It took every bit of willpower she possessed to remain standing, as if there wasn't some sort of magnetic pull shimmering between them. "Is that really what you want?" he asked finally.

"Yes. Please try to understand, this is my career we're talking about. You have no idea how hard I worked to get into this residency program." She took a deep breath and let it out slowly. "I need to achieve my success as a surgeon on my own."

"All right, then," he agreed slowly. "I'll do my best to treat you exactly the way I would any other resident on my service."

"Thank you." She tried to smile, but felt as if her face might break with the effort. Putting the kibosh on their friendship was the right thing to do. Not only because he was her boss on the trauma service but because their lives were completely different. What would he think if he knew the truth about Tristan? About her? The things she'd done?

He'd look at her differently. Judging her. Maybe even treating her differently. As if she weren't an equal to every other resident in the program.

She couldn't afford any distractions. Not now. Maybe not ever.

"See you at work, then," Jake said. He didn't

waste any time in leaving, shutting the door loudly behind him.

She closed her eyes against a wave of pain. Pushing Jake out of her life wasn't what she wanted, but it was the only solution she could think of.

With a sigh, she pulled out her cell phone and returned her family's phone calls.

Hannah stood at the podium in the three-hundred-and-fifty-seat auditorium, which was almost completely full, a sick feeling in the pit of her stomach. Just her luck, she was the first intern to be on first call, and now she was the first intern to present her patient at M & M rounds.

Her mouth was cotton-dry and she took a desperate sip of her water, willing the nervousness away. As medical students they'd had to present in front of large groups of people often enough that she'd pretty much become used to it.

However, today she would have to be prepared to respond to questions, and even though she'd studied up on Ehlers-Danlos syndrome until she could recite the pathology forward, backward and sideways, she knew she'd never be able to relax until this nightmare of a presentation was over.

"The first case this morning, Mr. Christopher Melbourne, will be presented by Dr. Hannah Stewart," Jake said, before stepping back and allowing Hannah access to the podium.

"Thank you, Ja—Dr. Holt." Mortified at her near slip in calling him by his first name in front of the entire surgical-services team, it took her a few moments to focus on her presentation. Hannah clicked on the first slide, where she'd summarized the basics. "Mr. Melbourne was a twenty-one-year-old patient who'd been diagnosed with Ehlers-Danlos syndrome at the age of seven. Ehlers-Danlos syndrome is a rare connective-tissue disorder that is hereditary. The classic signs of this syndrome are weak blood vessels resulting in numerous aneurysms."

As she spoke, some of her nervousness eased and she went through her slides, displaying Christopher's scans and using the lighted pointer to show the extent of his massive abdominal aortic aneurysm.

She went through a few more slides, and then finished with the events leading up to his death. "Mr. Melbourne was deemed not to be a surgical candidate, and his condition deteriorated from the moment he arrived in the ICU. We— I started CPR but almost immediately his father asked us to stop. His father also declined an autopsy." She forced herself to scan the faces in the crowd. "Any questions?"

A hand went up from one of the other attending physicians on the trauma service, Steven White. "Why wasn't he a DNR?"

She nodded, knowing the abbreviation meant "do not resuscitate." "Good question. Apparently his parents divorced shortly after the realities of the diagnosis set in, and Christopher's mother left them to deal with everything by themselves. He and his father were very close. His father knew the prognosis, and during several of Christopher's previous admissions the discussion of DNR was broached. Unfortunately, Christopher saw being a DNR as giving up and he continually refused to consider that option. He expressed a clear desire to have everything possible done to save his life and his father went along with his son's wishes. But in the end his father was the one to stop our resuscitative efforts."

Another hand went up and she inwardly groaned when she saw it was the chief of surgery. "Isn't there a new technique for repairing aneurysms that could have been attempted?"

She stared at him in dismay. She hadn't read anything about a new surgical technique for repairing aneurysms. Every physician in the room was staring at her expectantly and she wished the floor would open up and swallow her to save her from this awful humiliation. "Ah, I'm not familiar with the new surgical technique you're referring to." Helplessly she glanced at Jake, who was seated in the front row.

Several long seconds passed, and she began to get extremely worried Jake wasn't going to say anything. Especially after she'd basically told him the other day at her apartment that she didn't want any special favors.

Finally, he stood and turned to face the group. "There is a new technique for repairing aneurysms but unfortunately it was tried on a patient with Ehlers-Danlos syndrome at Mayo without success. I personally have used the technique in several cases but because Mr. Melbourne was so unstable, I decided the risk outweighed any benefit."

Feeling mortified that she hadn't known the correct answer, her research hadn't revealed any new surgical technique, she swallowed hard and kept her chin high. There were a couple more questions, ones she could address, about the details of the disease.

Finally, the ordeal was over.

There wasn't time to thank Jake for stepping in to help her as another intern had to report on a case. But

Andrea leaned over and whispered, "Good job," which made her feel a little better.

When the presentations were finished, she hung back, waiting for Jake, who was having a low conversation with Richard. Even though they hadn't spoken on a personal level since the scene at her apartment, she wanted to thank him for his help during the presentation.

Gregory Matthews, the chief of surgery, walked up. "Dr. Stewart, you're the resident who placed Mrs. Carmichael's central line, correct?" he asked, his expression serious.

The knot in her stomach tightened painfully and her mouth went desert-dry. "Yes, sir," she responded.

"I noticed she experienced a short run of V-tach during the procedure."

Once again, she wished the floor would open up so she could disappear. But one thing she'd learned early on was that admitting your mistakes went much further than glossing over them. "Yes, sir. In retrospect, I believe I put the guide wire in a little too far because I underestimated the impact of her small frame. I want you to know I did apologize to her for any discomfort I may have caused."

"Hmm." For a moment the chief stared at her, and it occurred to Hannah that this wasn't the best way to obtain the attention of the chief of surgery. Was her central-line complication the reason he'd asked such a difficult question during her presentation, putting her on the spot in front of all her superiors and peers? "Well, Dr. Stewart, I certainly hope you've learned from your mistake."

"Yes, sir, I have." A tiny part of her wanted some recognition for the way she'd handled the emergency, but obviously that wasn't going to happen. Get. Over. It.

"Good." Thankfully, he didn't say anything more about her skills or lack thereof. He turned away. She caught Jake's gaze and for a moment she thought he was going to come over to talk to her, but instead he called out to the chief, "Greg, do you have a minute?"

"Sure," he replied.

Deep in conversation, they walked out of the room together.

As she stood in the near empty auditorium, Hannah realized she might have acted too hastily in pushing Jake out of her life.

Because she'd never felt more alone as she did right now.

"I should have told you about the V-tach episode during the central-line placement," Jake apologized to Greg as they left M & M rounds, after hearing his discussion with Hannah. "Dr. Stewart did inform me of the event and I checked on Mrs. Carmichael afterward. Despite what happened, she had nothing but good things to say about Dr. Stewart."

"Yes, Eva said the same thing to me. She liked Dr. Stewart and was also very complimentary about you, as well." Gregory sent him a sidelong glance. "What's the matter—do you think I was too hard on your intern?"

Jake wasn't sure what he thought. Walking away from Hannah the other day hadn't been easy. He'd been stupid to give in to the impulse to kiss her in the first place, because one kiss and he'd nearly lost his head.

Trying to be Hannah's friend had backfired, and she'd

made it clear she didn't want any special favors, yet here he was, sticking up for her with the chief of surgery.

"Not necessarily. Ha—er…Dr. Stewart did make a mistake in judgement. I was called down to the trauma bay for two motor-vehicle-crash patients or I would have put the line in myself."

"Jake, I'm not blaming you," Greg said, slapping a hand on his back. "You know how important it is to keep these residents in line."

"Yeah," Jake murmured. But he didn't really believe it. Everything Hannah did was for the benefit of her patients. After that first mistake with the antibiotic, he hadn't found any other error. He could count on her to ask if there was something she didn't know, rather than try to bluff her way through it.

Of all the residents on his service, it wasn't Hannah who needed to be kept in line. His conversation with Richard Reynolds hadn't gone as well as he'd hoped. The senior resident had become extremely defensive when Jake had cautioned him against slacking off. Claimed he hadn't realized his pager battery had died.

Jake wasn't buying the age-old excuse—hell, even the interns knew better—but he let it go. For now.

"If you're not busy this weekend, we could take the yacht out again," Greg offered.

"Ah, sure," Jake managed, even though going out on the yacht was the last thing he wanted to do. Unfortunately, being on the boat would only remind him of the night he'd met Hannah.

After the way she'd kicked him out of her apartment, he was forced to admit she wasn't acting anything like Allie. And he was having trouble dissecting his feelings toward her. He liked her, and desired her. But he still didn't think a workplace relationship was a very good idea.

In some respects, he wished he'd never taken her back to the condo he'd happened to be borrowing from Greg that very first night they'd met.

He still had erotic dreams about their night together. And the intense kisses they'd shared since didn't help at all. Both kisses had been entirely his own fault.

"I'll call you," Greg said when the elevator dinged.

"Sounds good." He turned away, leaving the chief to get into the elevator alone, choosing to take the stairs instead.

Lost in thought, he headed up to the general-surgery floor. He wasn't on call today, but he needed to talk to Steven White about keeping a close eye on Richard Reynolds. He didn't trust the senior resident and it would be best to alert Steven to his concerns ahead of time.

But as soon as he reached the top floor, he received a page from the trauma room. With a sigh, he turned around to go back down to the first floor, knowing that Steven would be heading down for the trauma call. If he wanted to talk to him, he'd have to wait until after the trauma resuscitation.

He nearly ran straight into Hannah, who was coming up the stairs. For a long moment they stared at each other.

"Hi, Jake," she said, stopping in the middle of the stairwell. "I was hoping to find you."

His heart betrayed him by racing with anticipation. Idiot. He tried to keep his expression impassive. "What's up?"

She bit her lower lip, looking a bit uncertain. He found the nervous habit far too endearing. He found everything about her far too endearing. "I wanted to thank you. For coming to my rescue during M & M."

"Yeah, well, there's no need," he said in an abrupt tone. "I would have done exactly the same thing for any other intern. The decision to use an advanced surgical technique wasn't yours to make. Don't worry, I wasn't treating you any differently from anyone else." He moved as if to step around her.

"Wait." She reached out and lightly grasped his arm. He stared down at her slender hand, marveling at the warmth that her light touch brought forth, and once again he found himself wishing things could be different. "I also wanted to apologize."

Apologize? That distracted him from his turbulent thoughts. "For what?"

"For being rude. For throwing you out of my apartment. I know I handled things badly."

He hesitated, staring down at her and trying to read her enigmatic expression. Had she changed her mind?

And why was he even considering that possibility? When would he learn from his mistakes?

"I'm sorry," she said helplessly, when he didn't respond.

His initial reaction was to forgive her in order to put their differences aside. As ridiculous as it sounded, he missed spending time with her.

One of the biggest differences with Hannah, compared to Allie, was that he could talk about the specific details of his job with her. Hannah understood different surgical techniques, even if she still had a lot to learn.

He'd found himself opening up to her about some of their patients, too. Sharing a closeness that he never thought he'd experience again. Being in a new city and

hospital, he didn't have many friends. Which was probably why he'd bonded so quickly with her.

And he was grateful, that from what he could tell, she
hadn't blabbed about their night together. He couldn't
bear to be the fuel for the hospital gossip grapevine.

He needed to find someone else to bond with. Hannah
was off-limits. "Doesn't matter to me, one way or the
other," he said, pretending indifference. "I think you
were right, it is best if we keep things on a professional
level between us. Now, if you'll excuse me, I have a page
to respond to."

When her mouth dropped open in surprise, her eyes
full of hurt, it took all his willpower to turn and walk
away.

CHAPTER TEN

HANNAH headed home, feeling completely drained after Jake's abrupt dismissal.

At least she could take some measure of satisfaction from writing James Turkow's discharge orders. Seeing patients go home after undergoing major surgery and a difficult stay in hospital, including a stay in the ICU, was an awesome feeling. Those were the moments that made the long hours and stress worth every bit of effort.

Tomorrow, however, she'd have to write discharge orders for Devon, which meant he'd go straight to jail to await trial. And that depressing thought only reminded her of Tristan.

Her conversation with her brother hadn't gone very well but in the end she'd agreed to give him money, in the hope that he wouldn't resort to armed robbery again.

Being in debt with credit cards and then losing his job had gotten Tristan in trouble. Robbing the convenience store with a knife had been a stupid, desperate move. And now the odds were stacked against him. Who would give him a job with a criminal record in this tight economy?

Trying to push her depressing thoughts out of her

mind so she could enjoy a few hours of non-work-related activities, she walked from the subway stop to her warehouse apartment building. When she opened the door she was a bit startled to find Margie, her roommate, sitting in the kitchen, eating a salad.

Not that Margie didn't have every right to be there, but it seemed that more often than not, Margie stayed over at Bryan's.

To a certain extent, Hannah had grown used to living alone.

"Hey, Margie. It's been a while—how are you? How are things with Bryan?" She kicked off her shoes and shut the door.

"Good. Great, actually." Margie was a pharmacist, as was her boyfriend, Brian. She pushed her empty salad bowl aside and turned to face Hannah. "I have news."

Hannah dropped her backpack on the floor near the front door and crossed over to the kitchen area. The way her roommate was obviously wiggling her left hand drew her gaze to the flashy diamond sitting on her ring finger. It took a moment for the significance to register.

"Oh, wow, Bryan proposed? You're engaged?" Hannah squealed and rushed over to her friend's side to give her a huge hug. "Margie, it's beautiful!"

"Isn't it gorgeous?" Margie took a moment to admire her ring, along with Hannah. "He proposed last Saturday night. Of course, I accepted."

Saturday? Almost five days ago? "And you're just telling me now?" Hannah demanded with a mock frown, her hands on her hips. "What's with that?"

"I'm sorry, but I guess we just wanted to keep the news to ourselves for a little while." Margie's gaze seemed a bit guilty and it took her a few minutes for the truth to register. But when it did, she realized why her roommate hadn't immediately told her the news.

"You're moving out, aren't you?" she asked, dreading the answer.

Margie hung her head for a moment, and then nodded with a wince. "I'm sorry, Hannah. I know my timing sucks, but our lease is up at the end of August and you need to know I'm not going to renew. Bryan and I need to save money for our wedding, so I'm going to officially move into his place."

Hannah's knees went a little weak, and she dropped into the nearest kitchen chair, pasting a bright smile on her face to hide the depth of her despair. She couldn't blame Margie, and with a brief glance around the apartment she realized that over time Margie had slowly moved things over to Bryan's, to the point that the only items left were the overstuffed sofa and cherrywood end tables.

Margie and Bryan had obviously been planning this for a while. If she hadn't been so focused on her own problems, she probably would have figured it out sooner, instead of feeling like an idiot, being the last to know.

"I understand, Margie," she said slowly. "I guess I knew this day was coming eventually. You and Bryan have been joined at the hip for the past year." But she hadn't expected to deal with finding a new roommate or a new place to live quite this soon.

Even if she did find someone, she'd be forced to split the rent equally.

She drew a shaky breath and let it out slowly, trying to rein in her panic. First Tristan getting out on parole and now losing Margie as a roommate. Her financial situation was going downhill fast.

Less than two months. She had just over six weeks to work out new living arrangements.

"I'm sorry, Hannah," Margie repeated, as if sensing Hannah's true feelings. "I dreaded telling you, because I knew it would be difficult for you."

Hannah shoved her bout of self-pity aside. "Don't be ridiculous. Good heavens, Margie, you're engaged! I think this news calls for a celebration." She stood up and crossed over to rummage in the fridge. "Don't we have an unopened bottle of champagne left over from New Year's? Yep, here it is." She pulled out the bottle and proceeded to open it, shooting the cork right up into the ceiling with a loud pop.

Margie opened the cupboard above the sink and drew out two slender champagne flutes. "Let's fill them up," Margie said with a giggle.

Hannah poured the champagne and then lifted her glass in a toast. "To you and Bryan—may your marriage be filled with many years of happiness."

"Aw, thanks, Hannah," Margie murmured. "I'm so happy with Bryan. He's a great guy."

"Of course he is—you wouldn't settle for anything less," Hannah said supportively.

As Margie talked about their plans for a summer wedding, Hannah resisted the urge to down the entire glass of champagne in one gulp. She and Margie had been rooming together for the past six years, meeting in one of their undergraduate classes and being friends ever since. Their friendship had survived many ups and downs. The thought of starting over with someone new was overwhelming.

"I'll be out by the weekend. I figure I'll leave most of the furniture here for you," Margie said casually, "as Bryan has plenty of stuff."

"No, Margie, it's only fair you take what's yours," Hannah argued. It was easy to see that Margie was trying to ease her guilt by leaving all the furnishings. "I'll manage."

"It's not a big deal. Bryan has newer stuff anyway." Margie finished her glass as her cell phone rang. "Oh, that's Bryan now. He's coming to pick me up." After a brief conversation with her new fiancé, Margie rushed over to give Hannah another hug. "Thanks for not being mad at me," she whispered.

"Never," Hannah replied, returning her hug and hoping her misty eyes wouldn't be noticed. "Just promise me you'll be happy."

"I will!"

She managed to hold it together until Margie had left. Even though she'd stayed by herself in the apartment hundreds of times, the finality of Margie's leaving made the emptiness worse.

Hannah poured herself another glass of champagne and prepared to drown her sorrows.

"Okay, Devon, you're all set to go," Hannah announced, finishing the last of his discharge orders.

"I don't wanna go to jail," the nineteen-year-old whined.

At that moment he sounded exactly like Tristan. Four years ago Tristan had been the same age, nineteen, and he hadn't wanted to go to jail. Now her brother was free and she hoped he'd make good choices.

She gave him a stern look. "You tried to rob a liquor

store," she reminded him. "Call me crazy, but when you get caught breaking the law it shouldn't be a surprise to end up in jail."

"It was Joey's idea," Devon muttered with a sullen look on his face. He had a liberal sprinkling of tattoos over his arms and chest but thankfully none of the gang markings she'd come to recognize.

If he wasn't sucked into a gang, there might be a chance Devon could pull himself back on track. Of course, that's what she'd once thought about Tristan and so far that plan hadn't exactly turned out as she'd hoped.

"Devon, listen to me. You're the only one who can turn your life around," she said. "Not your brother Joey, not any of your other friends, only you. If you stay on the course you've chosen, you'll end up in and out of jail for the rest of your life. Or you could use this opportunity to turn your life round. Take the classes they offer in prison. Learn a useful skill, because getting a job with a criminal background isn't going to be easy. But if you believe in yourself, anything is possible."

Devon scowled but seemed to listen. She heard a noise outside the door and turned to find Jake standing there. His empathetic gaze met hers, and she realized he'd overheard her conversation with Devon.

She moved as if to walk past him, but he stopped her with a light hand on her arm. "Almost sounded as if you were speaking from experience."

With his face so close, and his gaze locked on hers, she couldn't lie. "Yes."

His eyes widened in shock but just then their trauma pagers went off simultaneously, announcing the arrival of another patient. The flow of trauma patients had been nonstop over the past few weeks.

She followed Jake, who took the stairs, the quickest route, down to the trauma bay.

Eleven in the morning should have been too early for motor-vehicle crashes, but that was the call on her pager. And when the four gurneys were wheeled in one right after another, her heart sank.

"What happened?" she asked, rushing over to the last patient being taken over to the farthest trauma bay. The patient was a sobbing child, who Hannah estimated to be in her early teens.

"A spare tire flew off the back of a pickup truck and smashed through the windshield of a van," Andrea said, before going over to the third patient.

Jake had taken over the care of the first patient, who looked to be the most serious of the bunch. The driver, no doubt.

"I want my mommy!" The young teenage girl sobbed as one of the nurses tried to offer comfort. Hannah pulled her gaze away from the driver, whom she assumed to be the girl's father, and began her trauma assessment.

"It's okay," Hannah soothed, taking precious seconds to try to put the girl at ease. "I need to examine you, okay?"

"BP ninety over forty-four with a pulse of one hundred and one. Respirations thirty," the nurse announced.

Stable vitals meant she could take her time in assessing for injuries. She didn't want to miss anything. She bent over to do a neuro exam, breathing a sigh of relief that the girl's pupils were equal and reactive. She'd get a head CT just in case, but there was at least one obvious femur fracture and she wanted to make sure there weren't any others.

"Give a five hundred cc bolus of LR to get her pressure up. And get X-Ray in here. I want to see films of her chest, pelvis and all extremities," Hannah ordered.

"What about her abdomen?" the nurse asked.

"A CT scan of her abdomen will give us more information than a flat film." She'd noticed that this was the same protocol that Jake tended to use. "Once I evaluate the status of her lungs, we'll get the CT scan."

"Okay," the nurse agreed.

"Where's my mommy and daddy?" the girl cried, again.

Hannah glanced down at the girl's name on the clipboard. "Emily, your mom and dad are in beds right next to you. We're taking good care of everyone, so try not to worry about anything right now, okay?"

"Is Eric here, too?" the girl asked, gripping her hand tightly. Hannah could only imagine how scared she must feel.

"Is Eric your brother?" Hannah asked, as talking seemed to help make Emily feel better.

Emily tried to nod, but they still had her strapped down to the trauma board so she couldn't move her head. "Yeah, he's a year older than me. I'm the youngest."

"Let me guess," Hannah said, releasing her hand so she could write down her assessment. "Fourteen?"

Emily's luminous brown eyes widened in amazement. "How did you know?"

"I was your age once," Hannah said with a gentle smile. "Okay, Emily, here's the X-ray machine. We need to take a lot of pictures, so you'll need to stay really still. Can you do that for me?"

"Yes," Emily whispered. "But my leg hurts."

"We'll give you something for pain. Do you have any allergies?"

Her expression clouded. "I don't know."

Hannah glanced at the nurse closest to the IV. "Start with two milligrams of morphine and watch for any sign of an allergic reaction. If she tolerates it well, you can go to four if she needs it."

She stepped back, out of the way, so the radiology tech could begin taking pictures. While she waited, she went over to call an ortho consult, and then went over to see how the rest of the family was doing.

Emily's father had clearly taken the brunt of the damage. His lower face was bloody and she'd bet he had a broken jaw at the very least. And as Jake was in the middle of placing an intracranial probe in his head, she surmised he'd sustained a bad head injury, as well.

Emily's mother and her brother Eric appeared to have multiple fractures, but so far they both were responding to questions. Clearly the father was the sickest of the bunch.

Emily's chest X-ray revealed a broken collarbone and a small pneumothorax. Hannah placed a small chest tube and then turned her attention to the rest of the films.

Emily's leg had sustained a compound fracture, and the bruising along her abdomen made her suspect a liver laceration. Since the rest of the injuries weren't that bad, she went ahead and ordered a chest and abdominal CT scan.

While she waited for Emily to return, she headed over to offer Jake her assistance.

He was talking to the neurosurgeon on call and

glaring at the monitor. "There has to be more we can do to bring his intracranial pressure down."

"You've already started the hypothermia protocol and given IV mannitol. At this point all we can do is wait. I have a bed ready for him in the neuro ICU."

She could feel Jake's frustration radiating from every pore in his body. His face was tense as he nodded. "Fine, we'll send him up.

"Do you need anything?" Jake asked when he saw her hovering nearby.

"Just for you to review Emily's CT—she should be back any minute."

"No problem."

The nurses scurried around getting everything ready, and soon Paul Scotland was being transported up to the ICU.

Jake came over when Emily returned, and reviewed the scans for himself. "She has a grade-two liver laceration, but otherwise everything looks good to me."

"Should we watch her in the ICU overnight?"

Jake hesitated, and then shook his head. "No, ICU beds are tight, and she'd only get bumped out later if someone more serious came in. Send her to the general surgical floor. Who's the intern on call tonight?"

"I am," Andrea said, coming over.

"Steven White is the attending, and I'll update him on everything before I leave, but I'll need you to keep an eye on her."

"I will," Andrea promised.

Jake gave a brief nod and walked over to check on Tracey, Paul's wife, and Eric, Emily's brother. Hannah tagged along, anxious to know what the rest of the family was facing. She was relieved to discover only

Paul's injuries were deemed to be life-threatening. The rest of the family would be sent to beds on the regular floor. Jake told her to make sure the family members' rooms, other than Paul's, were all together. She was impressed with his decision, knowing that they would do better if they were together. The floor nurses upstairs protested the extra work, but she refused to take no for an answer.

While they were waiting for the beds to be ready, she stood by Jake as he did his best to reassure the fourteen-year-old. "Emily, I'm not going to lie to you, okay? Your father has a serious head injury." Emily's eyes immediately filled with tears. "But try not to worry. We're going to watch him very closely in the ICU. He has a good chance of getting better."

Big tears rolled down Emily's cheeks. "I want my daddy," she sobbed.

"I know you do." Jake's eyes were bright and his voice husky as he took Emily's hand. "I promise you, we'll do everything to help him get better."

Only once Emily had calmed down did Jake finally turn away.

"That poor family," she murmured, as the transporters arrived to wheel the stable family members to their rooms.

"Yeah." He shook his head slowly, not embarrassed by his display of emotion. "Makes me thankful for what I have. Life is too precious to waste."

She couldn't help feeling a tiny flash of guilt. She hadn't been thankful for her family lately, had she? No matter how difficult things were, people were more important than money.

She could try taking out another loan, although she'd

already taken out loans for all her undergraduate and medical school tuition. Maybe she wasn't quite maxed out yet. Even with the loans she already had, she'd be paying off the balance in monthly payments in an amount mirroring a mortgage on a house for at least the next thirty years.

But so what? She hadn't gone into medicine for the money. She'd wanted to help people. The way Marilee McDaniel had helped her. The kind surgeon had spent hours at Hannah's bedside during the ten days she'd been in the hospital, because her mother had either been working or taking care of Tristan. Marilee had befriended her. Had arranged for her teachers to send her homework, so she didn't fall behind. And one night Marilee had helped her study for a biology test, encouraging her to study medicine since she loved science.

Marilee had shown by example how people were important. Money was easily replaced. People weren't.

Her mother had made a bad decision in marrying her loser father, but it hadn't been her fault she'd ended up with arthritis and was unable to work.

And if Tristan needed financial support to stay out of jail, she'd help him.

The trauma bay emptied out, and they walked toward the staff lounge to get out of the way of the cleaning crew.

"Jake?" she called, quickening her pace to catch up.

"Yeah?" He paused, glancing back at her over his shoulder.

Working with him, and watching him interact with this traumatized family, made her realize just how much he reminded her of Marilee McDaniel. And how lucky she was to have him as one of the surgeons teaching her. "I want you to know, I think you're an amazing surgeon."

Surprise bloomed on his features. And then he scowled, as if he felt uncomfortable. "I didn't do anything," he protested.

Throughout her four years of medical school training she'd discovered most surgeons had grossly inflated egos and personalities that tended to revolve around themselves. She'd rarely met any that showed the kind compassion of Marilee.

And Jake Holt.

"You did everything, and more." His humbleness only made her like him more. "I can only hope that someday I'll be even half as good a surgeon as you."

CHAPTER ELEVEN

JAKE stared at Hannah for several long seconds, wondering if he was dreaming or if she was really standing there telling him how much she admired him.

He searched her gaze, looking for a hint of the cold calculation he'd come to recognize in Allie.

But all he saw in Hannah's eyes was frank admiration.

"You remind me of a surgeon who operated on me my freshman year of high school," she continued. "She was amazing, going above and beyond while caring for me. She became larger than life in my eyes, and she was the reason I became a surgeon."

He was humbled that she'd compared him to this person who'd made such a lasting impression. "Sounds like she was something special."

"She was. And so are you."

He did his best to ignore an abrupt surge of desire. He cleared his throat and tried not to look embarrassed. "Trust me, you'll make a great surgeon, Hannah."

"I hope so." The bright, genuine smile on her face almost tempted him into grabbing her and kissing her until she couldn't breathe. But, of course, her pager went off. "Well, I guess I'd better go. Maybe I'll see you later?"

"I'll find you," he promised. For a moment their gazes locked, before she hurried away. He stared at her, knowing his resolve to stay away was sinking fast.

The way she'd tried to help Devon, when most people shrugged off gunshot-wound victims as getting what they deserved, humbled him. From what she'd described at breakfast, her life had been anything but easy. She was different from any woman he'd ever met. No matter how hard he'd tried to keep his distance, somehow he always gravitated back to her.

Suddenly he couldn't understand why he was trying so hard to abide by his stupid rule. Hannah wasn't Allie. She was a hundred times better than Allie!

Allie had deliberately schemed to land herself a surgeon. He'd heard her talking about it with another nurse and when he'd confronted her, she'd denied it, claiming she loved him. Yet when he'd broken things off with her, she hadn't wasted any time in setting her sights on another attending, Jeff Andrews, one of the orthopedic physicians. Right before he'd left Minneapolis, he'd heard they were engaged to be married.

No, Hannah wasn't Allie. She hadn't thrown herself at him in her apartment. And she'd kept their relationship a secret, instead of spreading word through the hospital.

As he walked back to his office, he realized that staying away from Hannah would be next to impossible. For one thing he liked her, admired her too much. And just being near her made him want more.

He wanted to spend time with her. Talk to her. Maybe

give a relationship a try. Take her out someplace nice, maybe a fancy dinner and a movie.

Make love with her again, if she was willing. Which she'd just given him the impression she was.

On one hand, he knew he was playing with fire. What if he managed to get burned, the way he had with Allie?

Yet he kept coming back to the differences between them. He wanted to believe Hannah was different. That she wasn't just handing him a line when she told him she admired him.

That she'd really meant what she'd said.

He couldn't stop thinking about Hannah when he should have been concentrating on finalizing his proposal for Gregory Matthews.

Dinner that evening with the chief went well and, best of all, Gregory approved both positions—the trauma program manager and the administrative/data-entry assistant.

His professional career was well on its way. At least he had all the changes on paper, even if the positions wouldn't be filled instantly. And soon they'd be able to implement the rest of the changes he'd planned. Chicago Care's trauma program was going to become the best in the country, if he had anything to say about it.

He was proud of what he'd managed to accomplish, but on a personal note he hadn't been able to spend even thirty seconds alone with Hannah. She'd smiled at him every time their paths crossed, so he didn't think she was avoiding him.

He was determined to spend at least a few minutes alone with her, but she was in surgery by the time he left for the evening. That night he kept waking up, annoyed to realize only a couple of hours had passed.

On Friday morning he headed to Chicago Care, surprised to notice the sky was filled with the threat of dark storm clouds. The humidity was so thick he could swear he felt the dampness of the air on his face. Obviously he hadn't been paying much attention to the weather lately, but the impending storm was actually a good sign.

The members of the knife-and-gun club, as ED staff generally referred to those who tended to settle their disputes with weapons rather than words, didn't come out to play as much when it was raining. Especially during thunderstorms. Which meant fewer potential trauma patients rolling through the doors.

A quiet day in Trauma meant he'd have the opportunity to talk to Hannah.

Yet his theory was soon proven wrong as the ED was hopping when he arrived. Since this was Steven White's week to be on call, Jake didn't have as many patient-care responsibilities. Instead, he'd scheduled several meetings with the hospital administrators on the upcoming budget and on the latest data from the patient-outcome database they had participated in. There were several areas in which Chicago Care could perform better as far as their patient outcomes were concerned, and he wanted to put some new infection-control practices in place.

With a sigh, he strode toward the administrative conference room. A day full of meetings was only going to make the time drag even more.

On days like this he wondered why he wanted to be the chief of trauma surgery. Truthfully, he was much happier taking care of patients and doing surgery.

He managed, somewhat successfully, to put Hannah out of his mind and to concentrate on work. When the meetings were finally over he planned to head back up to the ICU to see how things were going. And to find Hannah. But on his way up, he received a 911 page from the chief operating officer.

With a frown he headed back down to the administrative offices. The COO was a man in his middle forties by the name of Burke Calhoun.

"What's going on?" Jake asked when he noticed a handful of hospital executives gathered there.

"Have you been watching the news at all?" Burke asked in a grim tone.

"Ah, no, I haven't. Why?"

"We're going to activate a code yellow for an external disaster," Burke informed him. "The evening rush hour is a total mess. There's a forty-car pileup on the freeway thanks to the thick fog rolling in off Lake Michigan. We're hearing there are already half a dozen patients in the emergency department and we have to anticipate there are probably more to come."

Calling an external disaster was serious stuff, and hospitals didn't take such actions lightly. "What do you want me to do?"

"For starters, don't plan on going home anytime soon," Burke said dryly. "I want you to be in charge of triage, down in the emergency department. We're setting up the boardroom as the disaster command center."

Jake nodded and didn't waste any time getting back down to the emergency department. He'd participated in several disaster drills involving situations such as this one. Every hospital did.

But luckily they didn't often have to activate the

emergency-management system. He hoped their practice drills held up to the real deal.

When he arrived in the ED, he found complete chaos. He glanced around for Steven White, the trauma surgeon attending on call, as he should have arrived at the hospital by now, but didn't see him.

He found Sarah, the nurse manager of the emergency department, standing in the center of the arena, trying to gain control of the chaos.

"Okay, we need to set up a triage system here," he announced, and almost immediately the staff surrounding Sarah quieted down. "I want each of your nurses to team up with a resident to decide which patients go where."

He glanced around the area, making several quick decisions. "I want all 'red' patients, who are deemed critical, to be immediately transported up to the ICU. We don't have room to do full resuscitative care down here. 'Yellow' patients can be housed in here in the arena until we can determine which ward to send them to, and all 'green' patients, with minor injuries, are going to be shipped over to the clinic area. Send all available nurse practitioners and physician assistants over there to treat and release as many of the minor injuries as possible." He paused and then asked, "Any questions?"

"No, that sounds good." Sarah looked grateful to have a plan. "How many patients do you think we'll get?"

"I have no idea. All the area hospitals have been put on alert, though, so we aren't the only ones who will be getting casualties."

Sarah nodded and everyone fell into their assigned roles. He stayed in the center of the arena, ready to jump in when needed.

Jake saw Hannah briefly, and started walking toward

her to talk, but someone grabbed his attention. "Dr. Holt? There's a phone call for you."

He took the phone from the emergency department unit clerk. "This is Jake Holt."

"Jake? Steven White here. I'm sorry, but I won't be in for my call shift tonight."

Jake scowled. "Steven, we're in the middle of a code yellow, and we have dozens of patients coming in. I really need you."

"Yeah, I know, but I'm trapped in my car in the middle of the forty-car pileup."

Stunned, Jake didn't know what to say. "You're trapped in your car? Literally trapped? Dammit, Steven, are you all right?"

"It's bad out here, really bad." Steven's voice faded in and out, either from a bad connection or because he was injured more badly than he was saying. "I've never seen anything like it, Jake. I'm not in pain or anything, but that might be because I can't feel my legs."

Jake's fingers tightened painfully on the phone as he imagined how helpless Steven must feel. "You're going to be fine, Steven, do you hear me?" He refused, absolutely refused, to consider the worst. "Help is on the way."

"I can hear the sirens, but I'm afraid it might be too late," he said softly. And then the connection was lost.

Jake tried to call Steven back several times, but his colleague didn't answer.

Hannah glanced at Jake, sensing something was wrong. She finished triaging the last of the group of patients, and as there would be a lull in the activity until the next wave of patients arrived, she headed toward him.

"Something's wrong. What is it?" she asked in a low voice.

His eyes widened. "What makes you say that?"

She stifled a sigh. "Because I know you, Jake. I watched your face when you were on the phone earlier. I could tell something bad happened. So you may as well tell me the truth."

His gaze softened and he gestured for her to follow as he turned and headed for the staff lounge. She gently closed the door behind them to provide privacy.

"Something bad did happen. Steven White is out in the middle of the pile-up on the freeway," he murmured.

She sucked in a quick breath. "Is he all right?"

"I don't think so," Jake said. He scrubbed his hands over his face in a gesture she recognized he often used when he felt helpless. "He sounded hurt, said he couldn't feel his legs. And he was still trapped in his vehicle."

"Dear God." She could only imagine how difficult it would be for the rescue workers to get through the wreckage to find all the injured people. "I'm sure they'll get him out soon."

"I hope so. He has a wife and a two-year-old son."

Jake's grim expression tugged at her heart. The desolate expression in his eyes caused her to step closer, wrapping her arms around him in a warm hug. For a moment she thought he was going to pull back, as she was violating their agreement to stay apart, but then he clutched her close, burying his face in her hair.

The embrace carried a sense of intimacy that was far more intense than the night they'd first met and made love. Hannah didn't want to let him go, but they were still in the middle of the code yellow and their time wasn't their own.

When Jake loosened his grip, she gave him another quick squeeze and then stepped back. "Does this mean you're stuck here all night with me?"

A reluctant smile tugged at the corner of his mouth. "Yep, I'm the lucky guy stuck here all night with you."

Their pagers went off, announcing the arrival of six more patients. They'd already had word about how ambulances were bringing as many as possible on each trip.

"Let's go," Hannah said. "We'll keep an eye out for Steven."

"Yeah," Jake murmured, but she could still see the shadow of doubt in his eyes.

There was an odd hush in the arena as they waited for the patients, and then a sudden burst of activity as the doors from the ambulance bay opened. There were two ambulances filled with patients, and Hannah quickly lost track of time as the steady stream of ambulances continued to bring patients.

By midnight the stream had slowed to a trickle. The last patients to arrive were by far the sickest, including Dr. Steven White. He was on a long board, indicating a possible spine injury.

"What took you so long to get him out?" Jake snapped at the paramedic.

"We couldn't get the jaws of life in to open the car until we'd cleared a path," the paramedic responded.

Steven's face was pale and his eyes were closed as if he had lost consciousness.

"Get me a neurosurgeon over here—now!" Jake ordered.

Hannah stepped forward, hoping to calm him down.

"The neurosurgeon is working on the woman with the closed cranial trauma up in the ICU. Why don't we get a spinal MRI scan first so we know what treatment he needs?"

"Fine, get him in the scanner, stat."

"Jake?" Steven's eyelids fluttered open and he raised his arm to grasp Jake's arm. "Don't call my wife."

Hannah frowned and leaned closer. "You don't want her to know you've been injured?" she asked, not understanding. "I'm sure she's been watching the news, Dr. White. She'll wonder if you were on the road during the multiple car crash. She's probably worried sick about you."

"Don't call her," he repeated stubbornly. "Not until I know the extent of the damage. Not until I know..."

And then she understood. He didn't want his wife to know in case he might be paralyzed. The paramedics had confirmed that he hadn't been able to move or feel his legs since they'd extracted him from his crushed car.

"You know she'd want to be here with you, Steven, no matter what," Jake said in a low voice. And when Steven kept shaking his head, he finally relented. "But if you don't want us to call, we won't."

"Thanks." Steven's eyes slid shut. Moments later, the nurse wheeled him over to Radiology for his MRI scan.

The results of his MRI weren't as bad as they'd suspected. He had several broken vertebrae in his lower back but, from what they could see from the scan, the nerves in the spinal canal appeared to be intact.

Hannah watched as Jake gave Steven the hopeful news. "The paralysis should be temporary. As soon as the swelling goes down, you'll get your feeling back. It may take some time and some work on your part," Jake warned, "but the damaged nerves should come back."

"Are you sure?" Steven asked, his gaze skeptical. "Wheel me over to the computer screen so I can review the results for myself."

Jake let out a disgusted sigh. "Listen, Cole Johnson is the neurosurgeon here tonight, and I've heard he's finished with the patient in the ICU so he's on his way down. You can ask him, if you don't believe me."

Steven insisted on speaking to Cole, so Hannah quickly brought him over to Steven's bedside.

"We're going to wait a few days for the swelling to go down before we take you to surgery," the neurosurgeon said, after verifying what Jake had already seen on the MRI scan. "But there's no reason to think you won't make a complete recovery."

"Thank God," Steven whispered.

With a triumphant smile Jake handed over his phone. "Call your wife."

Steven grimaced but took the cell phone and made the call.

Relieved at the news, Hannah went back to work. Within the next hour they'd triaged all the MVA patients, and things quickly settled back to normal. As there were extra staff members who'd stayed during the disaster, she wasn't plagued by zillions of phone calls. Hannah gladly headed down to her call room at about one-thirty in the morning.

Using her key, she opened the door and suddenly felt Jake behind her. She took a deep breath to calm her racing heart. "Hey, you scared me," she chided.

"Sorry," he murmured. His gaze intently searched

hers. "Hannah, I know we agreed to keep things professional, but I can't seem to stay away. Would you reconsider and have dinner with me tomorrow night?"

"You mean, as friends?"

Slowly he shook his head. "No, Hannah. I want more than friendship from you."

The husky confession did nothing to calm her erratic pulse. And she couldn't say no. Because she couldn't stay away from him, either. "Yes, Jake. I'd love to have dinner with you. Tomorrow or any other night."

The smile that lit up his face made her heart stumble and trip in her chest.

She cared about him. A lot. Far more than she should. Logically she knew Jake had the power to hurt her, but she shoved the doubt aside. They might be from different worlds, or even different planets, but he wasn't like the rest of the attending physicians.

He cared about people. People like her.

And suddenly she didn't want him to go.

"Would you be interested in staying for a while?" she asked, pushing the door to the call room open in a silent invitation, nervously holding her breath.

But she needn't have worried. His green eyes flared with heat. "Are you sure, Hannah? I can wait if you're not ready."

"That's very kind, Jake. But I'm sure. Absolutely, positively sure."

CHAPTER TWELVE

JAKE followed Hannah into the call room, his heart hammering so hard in his chest he was surprised she couldn't hear it beating against his ribs.

For the first time since their initial meeting at Shipwrecked, it seemed they were both in sync, wanting exactly the same thing.

Hannah paused in the center of the room and glanced over her shoulder at him, a hint of uncertainty in her gaze.

He closed the door behind him and twisted the lock. He held her gaze, allowing the need he felt to show on his face.

Hannah's answering smile only made his heart pound more. There wasn't a speck of makeup left on her face, and they'd worked for hours on the disaster victims, but she still had the power to make his knees go weak.

"Hannah, you're so beautiful, you take my breath away," he murmured, approaching slowly, as if there may be a chance she'd change her mind.

She didn't. She met him halfway. And suddenly he understood that rushing into that one-night stand hadn't been to their advantage. In fact, that night together, while physically intense, had only complicated things.

They'd needed time to get to know each other, personally and professionally. Two weeks didn't seem like an incredibly long time, yet they'd worked side by side through numerous difficult situations, including this most recent disaster.

Under intense pressure, it was almost impossible to hide the true nature of a person's personality. Maybe if he'd worked with Allie this closely, he would have been clued in to the games she was playing sooner.

But this wasn't about Allie. It was about Hannah. And making sure she understood how much he wanted her. How much he cared about her.

The L word almost formed in his mind before he ruthlessly pushed it aside. He cared about Hannah, but he wasn't sure he was ready to love anyone. At least, not yet.

"I wanted you, Jake, the moment I saw you," she said honestly. "And leaving you the next morning was the hardest thing I've had to do in a long time."

Any lingering doubts about what they were about to do flew right out of his mind. He crossed the room, cupped her face in his hands and lowered his mouth to hers.

She let out a husky moan, kissing him back and pressing urgently against him, but he refused to be rushed. "Relax," he said between kisses. "We have plenty of time. Richard promised to keep an eye on the ICU patients for a while."

She froze and pulled away, her eyes wide with horror. "You actually told him I wasn't to be disturbed?" she asked on a choked gasp.

"No!" He didn't want anyone to know about their relationship, especially the people they worked with.

"I had a little heart-to-heart with Richard at the end of last week because I felt like he was slacking off. I think he's trying to make amends."

"Oh." The acute relief on her face was comical. Then she sighed. "I should stop trying to make this more complicated."

"Good idea," he said in agreement, kissing her again. Slowly. Gently. Drawing out the pleasure as much as possible.

As always, the sexual chemistry between them flared to life the moment they touched. But he held the surge of awareness in check, taking his time and exploring the depths of her mouth.

"Jake," she moaned, when he finally released her lips to explore the curve of her neck. She tugged at his scrubs, sliding his shirt up to rake her nails over his chest. He shuddered and swallowed a groan. "Please?"

Slowly, he reminded himself. He wanted to take things slowly. "Hmm, not yet."

"What?" she gasped, when he licked the enticing V between her breasts.

He chuckled and scooped her slim frame into his arms, placing her on the narrow bed. It wouldn't be as comfortable as his king-size bed, but it would have to do. He stripped off his shirt and helped her with hers, before stretching out beside her.

"There's no need to hurry," he advised, dodging when she reached down for the drawstring of his scrub pants. This would be over far too soon if he let her explore him. "I want to see and kiss every inch of you first."

She gasped and moaned when he bared her breasts. He couldn't help smiling a bit as he took a rosy tip into his mouth, suckling gently.

She cried out with pleasure and he hung on to his control with an effort. While the few hours they had seemed like an amazing gift, he knew that a few hours with Hannah would never be enough.

Never. He'd always want more.

He was killing her, Hannah thought as his mouth dropped to the region of her belly button.

Slowly and irrevocably killing her.

"Jake, please," she begged shamelessly. She didn't understand why he was holding back. "Stop torturing me."

His breath blew over her damp skin as he chuckled. "Torture? And here I thought I was pleasuring you."

"I'm going to die if you pleasure me much more," she said in a completely serious tone. "And it's not fair, because I want to pleasure you, too."

He glanced up at her, his gaze glittering with barely leashed passion. The intensity of his gaze made her suck in a harsh breath. This was so different from the first night they'd spent together.

Jake was different. More serious. More intent.

Some tiny part of her brain warned her there was more going on here than she realized, but that thought was quickly overruled by her hormones clamoring for more. She didn't want slowly, she wanted *him*. "Jake, I want you *now*. Please?"

Her plea must have gotten through because he stripped off her remaining scrubs and found a condom from heaven knew where, before pulling her close. She gasped on a wave of pleasure when he slid deep.

Finally!

But even though she was ready for the wild burst of

passion she'd experienced before, he continued to move at a snail's pace, with slow, deep, deliberate strokes that only increased the pleasure as he gazed into her eyes.

Her heart swelled with an emotion she didn't dare name as the tension grew more intense between them. She felt emotionally naked. Transparently exposed. She'd never experienced this level of intimacy with anyone before.

Only with Jake. Twice now with Jake.

When the overwhelming flood of desire couldn't be contained a second longer, he cried out her name in a guttural voice as the peak of pleasure toppled them both.

Her heart hammering in her chest, she closed her eyes and held him close, realizing she'd gotten far more than she'd bargained for when she'd invited Jake into her call room.

What they'd just experienced was far from one-night-stand sex. It was more, much, much more.

The real question now was: Where were they going to go from here?

Too bad she didn't have the courage to ask.

By the time her heart rate returned to normal, she gave in to the fatigue that pulled her under.

Her pager woke her about an hour later. She almost fell off the narrow bed before remembering she wasn't alone.

She fumbled through their discarded clothing, searching for the annoying device. And when she finally picked the pager up, her heart sank when she realized it was Jake's, not hers. And then her pager went off too, indicating the call was a trauma alert.

"Jake," she said urgently, when he didn't so much as

stir at the noise of their two pagers. Using the light from the phone, she quickly sought and found her undergarments, reminded of the night she'd tried to sneak away from him. She pulled on a scrub top, but then had to tear it off again, when she realized it was his.

After she finally managed to get dressed in the proper clothing she reached out to shake his shoulder. "Wake up. There's a motor-cycle-crash victim on the way."

"Grumph," he mumbled, turning over on the narrow bed. Good grief, was he always this difficult to rouse in the mornings? How on earth had he made it through his residency program?

"Seriously, Jake, you need to get up." She wasn't facing a motorcycle crash on her own. She shut her phone and turned on the bedside lamp, which only had a forty-watt bulb but still made her wince.

"I'm up," he muttered, finally swinging upright and blinking the sleep from his eyes. She tossed his clothing in his lap and he squinted at her. "Did you say MCC?"

"Yes. You have to hurry."

She couldn't help being impressed. When Jake woke up, he woke up quickly. In less than thirty seconds he was dressed and back in attending mode. "Let's go."

Had he lost his marbles? "You go first," she said, giving him a slight shove toward the door. "We can't walk into the ED together."

For a second he hesitated, but then gave an abrupt nod as he opened the door and left. She waited a full two minutes, giving him plenty of time, before heading out after him.

They were crazy to think they'd be able to keep

their relationship a secret for long. Especially if they continued sharing time together in her call room.

Since that was a problem she simply couldn't deal with right now, she shoved it aside and took a deep breath before entering the trauma bay.

They must have taken longer than she'd realized because the patient had arrived and Jake was already barking out orders. She noticed he tended to do that when he was tense.

She came up to stand next to him. "How bad is it?"

"Too early to say for sure, but he's holding his own at the moment."

Keeping her eye on the monitor, she watched as the staff quickly obtained blood, put in IV access and performed an overall assessment.

"Dr. Stewart, I need you to place an arterial line in this patient," he said.

She was taken aback by the formal use of her name—was that for Richard's benefit? But she quickly turned her attention to the patient. She didn't want to brag, but she'd become known as being an expert in arterial line placements during her ICU rotation as a fourth-year medical student. She'd never missed.

The nurse closest to the supply cart pulled out the sterile tray and she prepped the site. After donning sterile gloves, she felt for the radial pulse.

Except it wasn't there.

"I'm not feeling a pulse here," she said sharply. Glancing up at the monitor over the patient's head, the heart rhythm looked normal enough. "He's in PEA."

"Let's do a pericardial tap to rule out cardiac tamponade," Jake said calmly.

Feeling far from calm, she glanced up at him, silently

asking if he intended for her to do the procedure. He nodded. Since she still wore sterile gloves, she waited for the nurse to open a new, longer needle for her. Her stomach tightened. This was a procedure she'd watched several times but had never performed on her own. After twisting the syringe to the end of the needle, she used her left hand to find the dichotic notch and then gently inserted the needle. Tugging on the syringe plunger, she withdrew a full sixty milliliters of blood.

"His pulse is back," one of the nurses announced. Hannah couldn't help breathing a sigh of relief. She'd done it!

"Don't withdraw the needle," Jake advised, reminding her that the danger wasn't over. "We'll need to make sure we prevent this from happening again." He glanced at the nurse, Alice. "Call for a CT surgery consult—he must have damaged his heart and possibly his lungs during the crash."

Holding the needle as steady as possible, she twisted another syringe on the end and pulled back. This time she only withdrew ten milliliters. But she still didn't remove the needle, prepared to withdraw more blood if the patient continued to bleed into the sac around his heart.

She glanced over at Jake, unable to hide her curiosity. "How did you know it was a pericardial effusion and not something else, like a pneumothorax? There are many reasons for this guy to be in PEA, but you automatically picked the right one."

He lifted a shoulder in a half shrug. "It's the diagnosis that made the most sense. I could picture his chest hitting the handlebars of the motorcycle as he crashed. A tension pneumo was second on my list, but my gut was telling me that it was his heart. Doesn't matter that much because we would have ruled out all potential causes eventually."

Yeah, she thought, impressed, but ruling out all options would have taken precious time. Would that type of instinctive medical decision making ever come so easily for her? She certainly hoped it would.

Their patient had a broken left leg, but his neurological status was remarkably intact. She kept drawing back on the needle in his heart as she listened to Jake and the neurosurgeon on call talk about the risks for going straight to surgery. The patient's closed leg fracture would need to be addressed, but wasn't the patient's top concern at the moment.

"How much have you taken off in total?" Daniel Fischer, the cardiothoracic surgeon on call, asked.

"Seventy-five ccs," she responded.

He nodded. "Okay, I'll take him to surgery. But you're coming with me, until I'm ready to open his chest."

Hannah wasn't going to argue. In fact, she was thrilled to be able to follow the patient up to the O.R. with Dr. Fischer. It was a good hour and a half later before she went back down to find Jake.

"So how was it?" he asked with a tired smile.

"Awesome," she answered. "And the tear in the blood vessel was small enough that Dr. Fischer could fix it pretty quickly. Did I miss anything?"

"No, I checked on Steven and he's doing fine. We need to get ready for rounds."

She was shocked to realize that time had flown by so quickly. It was already six in the morning. It seemed like just a few minutes ago that she and Jake had been in the middle of the fog disaster.

The morning rounds went fine, and after they'd finished, she went back down to her call room to shower and change. When she came out of the bathroom dressed in jeans and a blouse, she was surprised to find Jake waiting there for her.

"Ready to go?" he asked casually.

Go where? "Ah, sure." She hid her confusion by gathering up her personal items and shoving them into her backpack.

"Your place or mine?" he asked, as she opened the door of her call room.

She paused and glanced back at him. "I was planning to go home," she said inanely. Alone, she silently added, but didn't voice her thought.

He must have sensed her hesitation, because he smiled. "Hannah, I'm tired and I'm sure you are, too. I don't have anything on my agenda other than a few hours of sleep. But we have plans to spend the evening together, remember?"

How could she forget? His dinner invitation had been a very nice surprise.

But she hadn't anticipated they'd spend the entire day together. What seemed so simple when they were alone became more complicated when they were out in public.

She told herself to relax and be glad he wasn't brushing her off after the intense lovemaking they'd shared. But she wasn't quite ready to return to his place. "Mine."

"Okay." He didn't argue. By tacit agreement, they walked out to the parking structure where he'd left his car.

"You should really take the subway," she chided, as he pulled out onto the road.

"To save the earth?" he asked with a dry laugh. "I didn't realize you were a tree hugger, Hannah."

They argued lightly over the issue of global warming as he drove to her apartment. Parking wasn't exactly easy to find, and his frustration made her laugh. "See? I told you we should have taken the subway."

He finally found a spot several blocks down and pulled in. "No, we should have gone to my place. I have reserved parking."

She rolled her eyes and reached for her backpack but, as before, he was quicker. He came around the car and fell into step beside her.

"I hope my car is okay here," he muttered.

Before she could try to reassure him, a familiar voice called her name. "Hannah? Is that you?"

She stopped and turned, her heart plummeting when she recognized Tristan. Or TJ, as his friends called him.

He was dressed head to toe in black with several new piercings on his face and huge tattoos along both forearms. Two of his buddies, also dressed in black, flanked him. For a moment she could only stare at him in shock, barely recognizing the young man.

Jail had obviously changed her brother. And not for the better.

Jake scowled and stepped protectively in front of her, as if she might be in danger. "Get lost," he advised her brother and his friends in a low voice. "We're not looking for trouble."

Tristan and his friends burst out laughing, as if Jake's comment was hilariously funny.

She glared at Tristan in a way that told him to back off.

Though when had Tristan ever listened to her?

Never.

"We're not lookin' for trouble, either—right, sis?" Tristan said in a purposefully loud voice. "Tell your boyfriend to back off. I need to talk to you for a few minutes. Alone."

Jake sucked in a harsh breath as he swung an incredulous gaze in her direction. "Sis?" he echoed in shock.

His reaction was exactly what she'd expected, and really she didn't blame him for it. How on earth had she thought this could actually work between them?

Very simply, it couldn't. They might share the same profession, but their personal worlds were on different planes of the universe.

Despite how she'd pulled herself out of that dark place where she'd grown up, her mother, and now her brother, held her back.

She couldn't ignore her brother. No matter how much she wanted to.

She yanked the backpack from Jake's grasp and flashed a tight, humorless smile. "I'm sorry, but I have to cancel our date. If you'll excuse me, I have some family business to take care of."

CHAPTER THIRTEEN

JAKE was stunned speechless when Hannah tossed her backpack over her shoulder and walked toward the guy and his friends, who all looked as hard-core as any gang members he'd ever seen.

Her brother?

He muttered a curse under his breath and stood with his arms crossed over his chest, unwilling to leave her alone with the three men who could easily be considered dangerous. Although probably not armed. Hopefully not armed. He only relaxed a little when her brother's two friends hung back, giving Hannah and her brother some privacy.

She'd mentioned that her mother, who had arthritis, couldn't work and lived in low-income housing, but why hadn't she mentioned her brother?

What else hadn't she told him?

And why did the question bother him so much?

He wasn't proud of the flicker of doubt that crawled over his skin. Yet he couldn't stop thinking of what other secrets Hannah might be keeping from him. He tried to focus his gaze on Hannah and her brother, who were speaking in low, urgent voices.

Arguing? He couldn't tell. Unsure what to think, he

shifted his weight from one foot to the other, waiting impatiently. He was surprised when she reached into her backpack, took out her wallet and handed him several folded bills.

Her brother shuffled through them quickly, counting the bills before he stuffed them into his black cargo pants pocket.

"Thanks, sis." Her brother gave her a halfhearted, one-armed embrace before turning back toward his friends. Jake dropped his arms and took a deep breath when the three guys headed in the opposite direction.

Hannah turned to face him. She lifted her chin but didn't say anything.

"Why didn't you tell me you have a brother?" he asked, finally breaking the silence and trying hard not to sound accusatory. She didn't understand how much he'd wanted to trust her.

Needed to trust her.

She shrugged. "It's not easy for me to talk about my family. You overheard me talking to Devon, didn't you? I told you I was speaking from experience. Tristan's experience. He was just released from prison. And as a result of the felony on his criminal record, he hasn't been able to get a job."

Prison. For a felony conviction. He tried not to look as shocked as he felt. No wonder she'd given him money. "That must have been hard on you."

She let out a harsh laugh. "Yeah, but worse for Tristan, don't you think? Listen, Jake, I'm tired and I really need some time to myself. I'll—uh—call you later, okay?"

Before he fully understood what was happening, she'd

swiftly unlocked the door to her building and disap-
peared inside, shutting the door firmly behind her.

Back at Gregory's condo, he tried several times to call
Hannah, but she wouldn't answer her cell phone. After
leaving one voice-mail message, asking her to call him
back so they could talk, there didn't seem any point
to leaving more. Still reeling from the abrupt turn of
events, he stretched out on his bed and stared at the
ceiling.

With all the problems in her family, he couldn't imagine how Hannah had managed to put herself through
four years of undergraduate training, four years of medical school and now a surgical residency program. Not
to mention financially supporting her family, too.

Knowing about her past and the hurdles she'd over-
come to get where she was today only made him admire
her more.

Yet he was bothered by the fact that she hadn't con-
fided in him.

Honesty was important. Especially after the way
Allie had lied to him, right from the very beginning.
He'd fallen for her, yet she hadn't felt the same way about
him. Instead, she'd made a fool out of him after they'd
broken up, spreading horrible rumors throughout the
hospital grapevine.

Yet, as upset as he'd been then, he felt even worse
now. Because he cared about Hannah. Had opened his
heart to her, only to wonder if he'd made another horrible mistake.

He got up and called Hannah again, hoping she'd pick
up. But she didn't. Maybe she'd already fallen asleep.

No, he didn't really believe that. The longer she went

without calling him, the more he knew she had no intention of calling him. Not later today.

Not ever.

Leaving so abruptly like that was her way of breaking up with him.

He cared about her, but she obviously didn't feel the same way about him. But unlike the situation with Allie, this one was mostly his own fault.

The sick sense of failure wouldn't leave him alone. The truth mocked him. Here he'd been comparing Hannah to Allie, and yet they couldn't be more opposite.

Hannah hadn't purposefully sought him out. She hadn't jumped into a relationship with him the moment she knew he was an attending physician. In fact, she'd pulled away.

Because she was ashamed of her past. Of her brother.

Yet he was the one who stupidly hadn't pried the truth out of her earlier. He'd overheard her conversation with Devon, their young prisoner patient, but he hadn't pressed further. He should have kept after her.

Reassuring her that nothing she could say would change how he cared about her.

Battling a wave of self-loathing, Jake gave up trying to sleep. He checked his cell phone, noticing with despair that she hadn't responded to his voice-mail message. Even if he decided to head back over to bang on her door until she let him in, he couldn't force her to talk to him.

While the idea held a certain appeal, he knew the result would be that Hannah would only listen politely while he said his piece before sending him on his way.

With a sigh, he settled down at his laptop computer and booted up the machine. At dinner the other night, Gregory had asked how his apartment-hunting was going. Jake figured it was well past time he found another place to live.

And as he'd arranged for another attending to cover Steven White's shifts for tonight and tomorrow night, because of his now nonexistent plans with Hannah, he had the rest of the weekend off.

Searching for a place to live might help keep his mind off the way he'd messed things up with Hannah. He started with the free advertising website that the general public used to offer places for sale or for rent. He didn't find much for sale, so he moved on to the rental section. He wasn't in a rush to buy anyway, as he didn't know enough about Chicago to know where he wanted to live. Renting would be easier and give him time to find exactly what he wanted.

Most of the ads were for roommates, but he wasn't anxious to share a place with anyone else. However, one particular ad caught his eye.

Two-bedroom loft apartment in former Brady Street Warehouse, on the corner of Brady and Webster, available for immediate occupancy: either to share or to sublet. Call 555-7810 if interested.

Surprised, he read the ad for a second time to make sure he wasn't dreaming. But he'd called Hannah's cell phone enough over the past few hours that he immediately recognized her number. It was her apartment all right. Hannah was either looking for a roommate or was looking to get out of her lease entirely.

A reluctant smile tugged at his mouth as he scrolled through the attached photographs. He'd only been inside her place that one time, and he'd been a bit preoccupied with kissing her, so he hadn't taken the time to look around. Now he found he was impressed with the eclectic layout of her apartment.

He tried one more time to call her, but again the call went straight to voice mail. So he stared at the photographs of her apartment and began to formulate a plan.

He'd find a way to force her to talk to him, one way or another.

Hannah sighed and crawled out of bed after sleeping only for a little over an hour.

Every time she closed her eyes she saw the shocked horror reflected on Jake's face when he realized the pierced, tattooed man was her brother.

Tristan couldn't have shown up at a worse moment. Although, really, would there ever have been a good time for Jake to meet him? She seriously doubted it.

She couldn't blame Jake for his reaction. Her world was far from anything he was accustomed to. Better to forget about what had happened. Forget Jake. Picking up her cell phone, she saw several missed calls from him on the screen. Her fingers hovered over the redial key until sanity returned.

Forget about him!

Her stomach rumbled with hunger so she set the cell phone aside and walked over to the fridge to find something to eat. She frowned at the mostly empty shelves. There was half a head of brown lettuce, a jar of pickles and a mostly empty bottle of champagne from when she and Margie had celebrated her engagement.

That was it.

With a sigh she closed the door, realizing that food wasn't going to appear on the shelves magically, as she'd given Tristan her grocery money for the next month.

Rummaging in the cupboard, she found a half-empty box of stale low-fat wheat crackers. They tasted like cardboard, but she ate them anyway, washing them down with water out of the tap. The sharp edge of hunger gnawing her belly eased.

The situation wasn't as bad as she was making it out to be. Certainly not as bad as when she'd been growing up. At least she could get free food at the hospital with her ID badge. So, if she really got desperate, she could always head back there to grab something to eat.

Even though going to the hospital on her weekend off wasn't high on her list of fun things to do, it was an option. Better than sitting around the apartment, staring at the four walls and going crazy. The first thing she'd done when learning of Margie's plans to move out had been to discontinue the cable service. It wasn't as if she had time to watch much TV anyway.

But no cable also meant not having internet access, either. She'd have to log on to her e-mail at work to check for any responses to her roommate advertisement. She'd asked Andrea to move in, but Andrea was living with her boyfriend and had declined.

Her gaze fell on her phone again. She sighed, knowing she couldn't avoid Jake forever. They worked together, after all. She needed to call him to let him know that their relationship, if that's what you wanted to call what they'd had, was over. She didn't really think he'd mind, especially now that he knew about Tristan.

Besides, she'd been crazy to think a lowly first-year resident could really hold the attention of a guy like Jake, who happened to be Chief of Trauma Surgery. They were at completely opposite points in their respective careers.

And in their personal lives, as well.

Tears pricked her eyes and she dashed them away impatiently. Her heart squeezed in her chest and she took several deep breaths to fight back a rush of desolation. This was ridiculous. She couldn't have fallen for Jacob Holt this quickly.

Yet somehow, illogically, she had.

She loved him. Loved Jake.

She sniffed and told herself to stop it. Since when did crying and wallowing in self-pity ever fix anything? She'd survive this, just like she'd survived working two jobs while going to medical school.

She just had to stop thinking about what she'd lost, that's all. And focus on what she had.

Determined to pull herself together, she rose to her feet and tossed the empty box of crackers aside. Time to get out of here. Maybe she would head to the hospital. Watch some trauma activity. Learn something.

Eat a decent meal.

When her cell phone rang she immediately thought the call might be from Jake, but instead there was an unknown number on the screen. Swallowing her disappointment, she answered. "Hello?"

"Hi, uh, I'm calling about the ad for the warehouse apartment."

The voice was oddly muffled, but she didn't think too much about it. She was thrilled that she'd gotten a response to her ad so soon, considering she'd only placed it yesterday morning before heading to work.

"That's great. Are you interested in subletting my lease?" The more she thought about it, the more she'd like to get completely out of the financial burden of the apartment. What if she didn't get along with the new roommate? Then she'd be right back where she'd started.

Besides, she'd already found a few potential places to live that were much cheaper. There were some tiny efficiency apartments that had caught her eye. Sure, she'd miss watching the sun rise over Lake Michigan in the mornings, but having food in the fridge would be nice, too.

"Yes. When do you think I could come and see the apartment?"

She hesitated, thinking fast. "I'm around this weekend, so you tell me what works for you."

"I can probably be there in about an hour."

An hour? So soon? She forced enthusiasm into her tone. "Great. I'll see you then."

The caller hung up so fast, she didn't have time to catch his name. At least, she thought the person on the other end of the line was a man.

Energized by the possibility of getting the place rented to someone else, she washed her face, hoping her red eyes wouldn't be too obvious, and quickly cleaned up the few items she'd left out. Margie had scrubbed the bathroom before she'd left, so that was good.

When the buzzer rang almost exactly sixty minutes

later, she released the lock. A few minutes later there was a knock at the door. She ran a hand through her blond hair and pasted a bright smile on her face before opening the door.

Her expression fell. "Jake? What are you doing here?"

He stepped inside, as if fearing she'd slam the door in his face. "Actually, I'm here about the apartment. We had an appointment, remember? Do you mind if I take a look around?"

Her jaw dropped in shock, but he appeared to be serious as he gazed around the open-concept living area intently. She couldn't think of a single thing to say when he crossed over to glance out of the large windows.

"Nice view," he murmured.

She crossed her arms over her chest and narrowed her gaze. Why was he doing this? As a joke? She wasn't in the mood. "You know very well your view is better. Be serious, Jake. You're not interested in renting an apartment. You already own a fancy condo."

He glanced over his shoulder at her. "The condo isn't mine. It belongs to Greg Matthews. He's letting me stay there until I find a place of my own."

The glass-and-chrome condo she'd hated on sight belonged to the chief of surgery? Seriously? She stared at him, unable to judge whether or not she should believe him.

But again he looked around, as if he was seriously considering renting the place. When he walked into the kitchen and opened the fridge, she tried not to wince.

"The appliances obviously stay with the apartment," she said hastily.

"Hmm." Thankfully he didn't say anything about

the barren state of her fridge, but continued mosey-
ing around. He looked inside every single cabinet and
drawer.

It felt very odd to have Jake snooping around her
home.

"Two bedrooms upstairs?" he asked, gesturing to the
open staircase.

"Um, yes. Feel free to go on up to look." No way was
she going anywhere near her bedroom with him there.
It was hard enough to keep the conversation between
them neutral.

She was oddly disappointed that he seemed to be
truly interested in the apartment. Or at least he was
giving a mighty good impression of being interested.

He was acting as if their night together had never
happened.

The same night she couldn't get out of her memory.

"Thanks." He went ahead and climbed the staircase.

She strained to listen as he went into each room.
Margie's was completely devoid of any furniture so his
steps were easy to trace as he moved across the hard-
wood floor.

Closet doors opened and shut. More footsteps.
Another peek into the bathroom. He was certainly covering all the bases, wasn't he? She didn't know what to
think. Finally, he came back down to the main level.

"I'll take it."

"Excuse me?" Surely she hadn't heard him correctly.
Had she? Jake was the chief of trauma surgery. There
had to be zillions of places for him to live.

Fancier places. Like the glass-and-chrome condo that

she'd assumed was his but wasn't. Surely there was some condo for sale, somewhere?

"It's a great place, nice and roomy. The open concept is awesome. I'll take it."

CHAPTER FOURTEEN

FLUSTERED, Hannah stared at Jake. He hadn't even asked about the rental. Then again, maybe he'd already called the leasing company to find out all the pertinent information. "Ah, okay. Great. That's really...great."

"Would you mind if we grabbed some dinner while we hammer out the details?" he asked, his impersonal tone making her feel as if they were acquaintances rather than former lovers. His carefree attitude grated on her nerves like nails raking down a chalkboard. "I'm starving. I haven't eaten in hours, and by the emptiness of your fridge, I'm certain you haven't, either."

"Uh, sure." Was Jake assuming they were picking up where they'd left off? Or was he going to find a nice way to break up with her? The thought made her feel sick, but it was better to have this conversation now, when they wouldn't be working together over the weekend, than later.

Just because she'd felt as if her heart had been ripped out of her chest, it didn't mean she couldn't pretend everything was normal.

She'd had plenty of practice pretending her life was normal over the years. It was how she'd survived high school, college and medical school. Sharing a quick meal with Jake wouldn't be any different.

"I passed a small Italian restaurant just a few blocks down the road that looked good," Jake said. "Are you willing to give it a try?"

She knew exactly where he was talking about. "Antonio's has great food," she said, heading for the door.

"Oh, so you've eaten there before?" he asked, as they waited for the elevator.

"Yes." Feeling awkward, she stepped inside and stared at the elevator door as they rattled their way down to the main level. "I've lived here for over six years."

"Six years? Really?" Jake's brows shot up in surprise. "Did you do your medical school training at Chicago Care?"

"No, I was in the University of Chicago's medical school program." Why did she suddenly feel as if she was talking to a stranger? It was downright mortifying to realize how much she and Jake didn't know about each other.

No wonder their relationship hadn't worked out.

Outside on the sidewalk she hesitated, wondering if he'd driven his car. Did he realize parking here was a nightmare? There was a reason she didn't have a car, other than the fact she couldn't afford one. Should she point out the lack of parking? Would he change his mind about taking over her lease if she did?

The idea shouldn't have cheered her up, but it did.

"It's a nice night for a walk, don't you think?" he asked, as if reading her mind. "Antonio's is just a couple of blocks north of here."

She knew very well where it was, but didn't say

anything as she fell into step beside him. Their fingers brushed and she immediately moved farther away, giving him more room. She felt his gaze on her but she stared straight ahead, refusing to make eye contact.

A strained silence hovered until they got to the restaurant.

"Hannah, how are you, dear?" Mrs. Antonio, otherwise known as Gina, met her with an enthusiastic hug. Hannah had done a stint of waitressing at Antonio's in her early years of undergraduate studies, but while it was a very nice place to work, the tips she'd earned hadn't been enough to live on. Not like the tips she'd earned at Satin, the gentleman's club. Of course the skimpy waitress outfit and the ass-grabbing had been the reason the tips had been high.

"I'm good, thanks, Gina. This is a friend of mine, Jake Holt. Jake, this is Antonio's wife, Gina."

"A friend, eh?" The way Gina looked at Jake with frank approval, Hannah could tell the restaurant owner was already assuming they were more than friends. Thankfully, the small restaurant was busy enough that Gina couldn't stay to chat, but quickly took them over to a small table in the corner, sending Hannah a sly wink as she hurried away.

"Would you like a glass of wine, Hannah?" Jake asked as he perused the menu.

"No, thanks." Wine would definitely make this casual conversation seem like a date. And it certainly wasn't.

"Come on, I'll order a bottle for us to share. I'm in the mood to celebrate."

She shrugged and offered a weak smile. Too bad she wasn't in the mood to celebrate, as well. Although she should be. At least she'd be better off financially now that she wouldn't be solely responsible for the lease.

So why did she feel so miserable?

She waited for Jake to finish reviewing the menu, because she knew it by heart and was already planning to have her favourite: spaghetti and meatballs.

Once they'd placed their order, Jake settled back in his chair and lifted his wineglass in a toast. "To new beginnings," he said.

"Absolutely," she murmured, wishing she felt as encouraged as he did, lightly touching the rim of his glass with her own before taking a sip. The red wine was incredible, and she had to resist the temptation to down the entire contents in a single gulp.

Jake stared into the depths of his glass for a minute before meeting her gaze. "I came to Chicago Care to make a fresh start. I was in a relationship back in Minneapolis with a woman whose only goal was to marry an attending physician. It was all about the status symbol, not real feelings."

She sat back in her chair, surprised by the revelation.

"In a lame attempt to protect myself, I decided not to date anyone I worked with because after I broke up with Allie, she made sure the entire hospital knew what a bastard I was."

"No, Jake." She wasn't buying it. "Anyone who really knew you would never believe that."

A ghost of a smile played along his lips. "Thanks, Hannah. But I probably deserved a little of the gossip for being such an idiot in the first place. But that's not the point."

It wasn't? She held her breath, bracing herself for the

worst. Now he was going to tell her why a relationship between them would never work.

As if she didn't know already.

"I haven't been fair to you, Hannah. I should have told you the truth a long time ago. I sincerely regret giving you the impression I was ashamed to be with you."

"You didn't," she protested.

His gaze was thoughtful. "Yeah, I think I did. I know you thought I was upset to find out you had a brother, but that wasn't really the problem."

Confused, she stared at him. "You don't have to explain, Jake. I get it. Tristan has made some mistakes, no question about it. And I'm hopeful he's learned from them. But I can appreciate that he's not the type of person you'd choose to be around."

His eyes flashed with anger. "Stop it. Maybe we started this relationship a bit backward, but I should hope you'd know by now that I'm not a snob. Your brother is family. I get that. I was only upset that you didn't confide in me sooner. Then I realized it was my own fault for keeping our relationship a secret. For acting like we had to sneak around." He sighed and jammed his fingers through his hair. "Well, I don't want to sneak around any longer."

"You don't?" she said, her heart grasping the ray of hope. Then she frowned. Was he really saying what she thought he was saying?

"No, I don't. Hannah, I'm asking you to give me another chance. I promise things will be different this time."

Stunned, she could only gape at him. Never, in her wildest dreams, had she expected the conversation to head down this path. She wondered if her sleep-deprived brain was tricking her.

Did he really want another chance? To be with her? Why?

Before she could think of a suitable response, or *any* response really, their food arrived. She dug thankfully into her spaghetti and meatballs. which normally tasted divine. Tonight she could have been eating sawdust.

"So, what's your timeline on the apartment?" Jake asked, abruptly changing the subject. "Do you already have a new place selected?"

She felt a little as if she was swimming blindly in the lake. One minute he was talking about a second chance, the next he was back to the subject of her apartment. "Not exactly, but I'm happy to work around your schedule. If you want to take over on the first of August, I'm sure I can find someplace else to live by then."

"I'm assuming your roommate moved out?" he asked.

"Yes. Margie is a pharmacist and she just finished her doctorate. She's getting married and she and Bryan, her fiancé, decided to move in together." Why she was explaining all of this to Jake, she had no idea. She was still reeling by the idea that he wanted a second chance.

She must have heard him wrong.

"I see. I'd like to move in as soon as possible, but if you need another month to find someplace to live, I'd be happy to pay the first month's rent anyway, and wait at the condo until you find what you need."

Her gaze shot up to his. Pay the first month's rent? Why would he do that? "I don't need your charity, Jake."

"It's not charity, Hannah," he responded. "It's more like a security deposit."

She wasn't fooled by his attempt to be nice. "No,

thanks. August first is fine. I'm sure I'll find something by then."

He surprised her further by reaching across the table to take her hand. "Hannah, I'm serious. Take the advertisement off the internet. I'll take the apartment when you're ready. There's no reason for you to rush into anything."

It was on the tip of her tongue to point out he'd rushed into the decision of taking over the lease of her apartment, but decided not to go there.

After all, she wasn't much better. Hadn't she rushed into their relationship? From the moment they'd met and she'd gone back to the condo with him she'd let the moment of intense attraction cloud her brain.

Really, she had no one to blame but herself.

She concentrated on finishing her spaghetti and meatballs, as if her world didn't feel as though it was falling apart.

"At least think about staying in the apartment for a while," he advised as he waved to their server, signaling for the check. "Give yourself time to think about where you'd like to live."

She could only nod helplessly, knowing she'd be unable to think of anything but his offer on the apartment and his request for a second chance.

A week later, Hannah found a very small efficiency apartment that was cheaper than her half of the rent would be if she stayed in her current apartment with a roommate.

The group of efficiency apartments happened to be located farther from the nearest subway station, but she'd survive getting up an hour earlier each day.

But when it came time to sign the lease for an August-first start date, she couldn't do it. Instead, she told the manager she needed time to think about it.

What was wrong with her? She didn't need Jake's charity, and no matter how he tried to disguise his offer, that was exactly what it was.

As she came up from the subway to street level, she realized it was raining. She ducked her head and ran toward her apartment building.

And practically collided with Tristan.

"Hey, sis," he greeted her.

As before, her stomach clenched when she saw him. She loved her brother, truly, but she didn't have any more money to give him. At least he was alone this time. She forced a smile. "Hey, Tristan. How are you?"

"Good. Really good." He seemed uncharacteristically happy. "Guess what? I landed a job."

For a moment she could only stand there, rain soaking her hair and running down her back as his startling news sank into her brain. "You did?"

"Yeah. You know how I'm always working on cars, right?" When she nodded, he continued, "Well, the guy who owns the garage on Fifth and Elm has some sort of medical problem that makes him unable to do the work himself so he hired me as his mechanic. I start on Monday."

Hope filled her heart and she smiled broadly. "Really? Tristan, that's awesome."

"Yeah, well, I wanted you to know. I've been hearing from Mom how hard you're always working, and how much you're always helping her, and that made me realize that I needed to get my act together if I want to stay out of jail."

Really? And here she thought her mother resented the hours she put into her career. Shame burned insisde her as Hannah realized that some of her issues with her family were her own fault. Vowing to be a better daughter, she threw her arms around her brother, giving him a bone-crushing hug. "I'm so happy for you, Tristan. Seriously happy for you."

Without his friends nearby watching, he returned her hug with equal enthusiasm. "Me, too. Thanks, sis. For everything."

Tears mixed with raindrops on her face, but she didn't care. She felt as great as if she'd been handed a winning lottery ticket with his news. "You're welcome."

Her brother left and she ducked into the building and out of the rain, shivering a little as she rode the elevator up to her apartment. Despite being soaked to the skin, she felt better than she had in a long time.

Maybe the fate of her family didn't rest solely on her shoulders. And even if it did, wasn't her family worth it?

Yes, they were.

And maybe Jake was worth a second chance, too.

Jake ignored the rain as he balanced the oversize box he held and buzzed Hannah's apartment.

"Yes? Who is it?"

"Me, Jake."

"Ah, sure. Come on up." She sounded surprised, even though he'd mentioned the possibility of storing some things at her apartment when they'd worked together yesterday.

Had she changed her mind about moving? He sincerely hoped not. He liked the layout of the warehouse apartment. When she opened the door for him, he flashed a quick grin. "Hi, Hannah," he said, as he set the box down inside the doorway.

"I didn't expect you to move any boxes today, in the rain. It's supposed to be sunny tomorrow."

"I don't mind," he assured her. Deep down, he knew he was using the boxes as an excuse to see her alone. Outside work. They hadn't had a lot of time to talk over the past few days. And he missed her.

"I found a place to live," she said. "And the good news is that it's available starting August first."

Something in her tone was off—the cheerfulness didn't match the resigned expression in her eyes. "Hannah, I was serious about my offer to pay the rent next month, so that you could have time to find something you really want."

"I already told you I refuse to be a charity case," she said, crossing her arms over her chest and lifting her chin stubbornly.

"And I told you, it's more like a security deposit. Greg isn't charging me for the condo, so why shouldn't I pay the first month's rent?" he argued.

"Stop it, Jake," she said wearily. "Stop the pretense. I wanted you to treat me like an equal, not as someone you need to rescue."

Appalled by her assumption, he slowly shook his head. "Hannah, you misunderstood my intentions."

"Really? And what exactly was your intention?"

Faced with her blunt question, he forced himself to be honest. "Our month together on Trauma is just about over. I was using the apartment as an excuse to keep seeing you."

Her eyes widened in surprise. "Why?"

"I asked for a second chance, Hannah," he said testily. "What did you think? That the time we've spent together was just a one-month fling?"

"You were serious about that?" Seemingly stunned, she sank down on the sofa. "I thought maybe that was just something you said after discovering the truth about my brother."

For a moment he suppressed a surge of panic. Had he made the same mistake of falling in love with someone who wasn't capable of loving him back? "I didn't change my mind," he said slowly, coming over to sit beside her on the sofa. "I was trying to give you time to understand your own feelings."

Seeing the hopeful expression in her eyes gave him the courage to see this through. Hannah wasn't Allie. Every moment he spent with her convinced him of that.

And he refused to deny the depth of his feelings. "I love you, Hannah."

"What?" The dazed expression on her face nearly made him laugh. Except that he wasn't sure how she felt about him. "H-how is that possible? You barely know me. We only met four weeks ago."

He knew her, better than he'd ever known Allie. Hannah was everything he wanted and more. "I couldn't take my eyes off you the moment we met. And even though I tried to stay away from you, I couldn't. What I feel for you is so much more than what I thought I had with Allie. This is the real deal, Hannah." His gaze bored into hers, willing her to understand. "I admire you. Your strength, your determination. The empathy you have for our patients. I honestly know I don't deserve you, but I am telling you the truth. I've fallen in love with you. I'm asking for a chance to show you how much I care."

"Jake, there are some things you don't know about me." The fearful expression in her eyes tugged at his heart. "Things that might change how you feel toward me."

He expected the familiar betrayal, but it never came. And suddenly he knew that no matter what secrets she had, they couldn't possibly change how he felt about her. "I don't think so," he said calmly.

"I was arrested when I was sixteen years old. For stealing."

"Yeah, so what? You were just a kid." Did she honestly think that bit of news scared him? "Hannah, I was hardly an angel as a kid. And what difference does it make what happened ten years ago? Look where you are now. You're the hardest-working intern on service. Even the other trauma attending physicians have commented on your work ethic."

"But…" She stared at him, confusion mirrored in her gaze. "Don't you even want to know what I took?"

"Hannah, it doesn't matter. Nothing you can say will make me change how I feel about you." He knew how he felt, but he wished for some sort of sign from her to understand where she was coming from. Was she looking for a way to let him down gently? He was determined to get the second chance he'd asked for. "I know you might not return my feelings yet, but I'm willing to be patient. To give you the time you need. Because I love you and I know that together we can make it work."

"Clothes. I took clothes from a department store." She acted as if she hadn't heard a word he'd said. "I knew shoplifting was wrong, but the popular kids kept teasing me about the holes in my clothes so I gave in to a moment of weakness. I got caught, of course, but the cops were pretty decent, all things considered. They could have put me into juvenile detention, but they didn't."

"Dear God, Hannah," he murmured, appalled at her story. "I'm sorry you had to go through that." And he could imagine that wasn't the only hardship she'd faced.

"They put me in a special high-school program that saved my life. For one thing, I wasn't near all those pretty, popular pom-pom girls who hated me. And I managed to graduate with honors and get into college."

"You make me feel like an underachiever," he admitted. And it wasn't a lie. For Hannah to get through that and accomplish what she had so far was nothing short of a miracle.

"No, don't you see? It's why I feel so bad about Tristan. For years I've thought it might be my fault that he took the same route as I did. Stealing. And like me, he got caught."

"Hannah, your brother is responsible for his own actions, just like you were."

"Maybe," she said uncertainly. "I just saw him, and guess what? He has a job. I'm so happy for him."

"That's wonderful news, Hannah." He gave her an exuberant hug, truly thrilled for her. "I'm happy for him, too."

"You really don't resent the fact that he's an ex-con," she said in a surprised tone.

"No, I don't." And he wished there was some way to make her believe in him. In what they shared. "And I'll tell you that a hundred times more if that will help you to believe me."

For several long moments she stared at him. "You're right, Jake. You've made me realize how I've used my past, and my family's troubles, to push people away who try to get close."

So was that good? Or bad? "It's understandable, Hannah. But I'm asking you to please give me a chance."

A smile bloomed on her face. "Of course I will, Jake. I want a second chance, too. Because I love you. I've loved you from the moment you came down to my call room after we lost Christopher. But I am a little afraid. I have such a long residency ahead of me and you're in a completely different place. I don't want to rush into anything. What if we don't make it?"

"Wait a minute—back up." He wasn't sure he'd heard her correctly. "You love me? Really love me? Are you sure?"

She laughed and nodded, tears glistening in her eyes. He loved the way she wasn't afraid to let her emotions show. "Yes, Jake. I love you. I think I'm the luckiest woman in the world to have found you."

He swept her tightly into his arms. "Thank God," he murmured against her hair. And in that moment he knew—everything was going to work out.

She pulled away, just enough to look up into his eyes. "Jake, you know this isn't going to be easy, right? I have a long haul ahead of me. Five years of residency plus a fellowship."

He kissed her hard and quick, and then raised his head. "Yes, Hannah. I do realize *we* have a long road ahead of us. But it doesn't matter, because I'm in this for the long haul. And you know as well as I do that anything worth having is worth fighting for. Isn't that why you chose to become a surgeon? There were certainly easier pathways to take if you only wanted to be a doctor."

"You're right, Jake. And I really do love you," she said in a serious tone. "More than you'll ever know."

"I love you, too, Hannah," he murmured before lowering his mouth to capture hers in a long kiss.

He planned to fight for Hannah. Now and always.

EPILOGUE

Eleven months later...

HANNAH couldn't believe she'd made it through her first year as an intern. Standing at the welcome reception next to Jake, she watched the new group of interns milling around with a sense of amazement.

Not too long ago she'd been as green as they were. It was incredible how much she'd learned over the past year.

Of course, there were times she'd wondered if she'd make it. But she always had Jake there, cheering her on. Coaching her. Mentoring her.

Loving her.

Not that he'd given her any special favors, but just having him there to talk to after a difficult night on call was more than she ever could have asked for. Having someone supportive at home, being there no matter what, was something she'd never experienced. She'd always been the strong one in her family.

She wasn't sure she'd be standing here right now if it weren't for Jake. And not because he'd spent hours helping her study for her boards.

Which she'd passed—her scores amongst the highest in the top quartile for the entire program.

"Almost ready to go?" Jake asked in a low voice. He'd made dinner reservations at Antonio's, which had quickly become their favorite Italian restaurant. And even though she'd moved into her tiny efficiency apartment, she'd spent more nights at his place than she did at her own.

"Sure." She glanced at him curiously, still somewhat amazed that the handsome chief of trauma surgery loved her.

There were times she still pinched herself to make sure she wasn't dreaming.

By mutual agreement, they took the subway to Antonio's. Inside, Gina and Antonio greeted them like lost children they hadn't seen in ages, rather than mere weeks.

"I have your table ready and waiting for you. Come! Sit! You'll have wine, yes?"

"What's up with them?" Hannah whispered to Jake once their wine and dinner had been ordered. "I've never seen them like this. It's like they've both been doing speed or something."

Jake smiled, took a sip of his wine and shrugged. "Beats me. I just hope it doesn't affect the meal. I've been looking forward to this all day."

She laughed and shook her head. "Men are so simple," she teased.

Suddenly, a small Italian man, who looked old enough to be Antonio's father, came over with a violin. He stood right next to Hannah and began to play a soft, romantic melody.

She was a little surprised as Antonio's didn't offer

music on a regular basis, but she sat back, enjoying the song.

Jake stood and came around the table, dropping to his knee in front of her. For a moment she didn't get what was going on. Until he opened the tiny square velvet jewelry box and handed it to her.

"Hannah, you've made it through your toughest year as a resident, and I still love you, more now than ever before. Will you do me the honor of marrying me?"

Tears sprang to her eyes when she saw the beautiful diamond pendant inside. It wasn't a ring, because surgeons didn't wear rings while they were operating. Plain gold bands would suffice. Touched, she brought her gaze up to his and smiled. "Yes, Jake. I'd be happy to marry you."

Gina and Antonio and the rest of the restaurant staff burst into applause. Shyly, she waited for Jake to place the diamond pendant around her neck.

"I love you, Hannah. You're going to be a great surgeon someday."

"Only because I had a great teacher." Ignoring the whistles from the other patrons, she pulled him close and planted a firm kiss on his mouth. "I love you, too, Dr. Holt," she whispered.

"My heart is yours, Hannah," he promised. "Now and always."

She smiled. She could live with that. Forever.

* * * * *

AUGUST 2011
HARDBACK TITLES

ROMANCE

Bride for Real	Lynne Graham
From Dirt to Diamonds	Julia James
The Thorn in His Side	Kim Lawrence
Fiancée for One Night	Trish Morey
The Untamed Argentinian	Susan Stephens
After the Greek Affair	Chantelle Shaw
The Highest Price to Pay	Maisey Yates
Under the Brazilian Sun	Catherine George
There's Something About a Rebel...	Anne Oliver
The Crown Affair	Lucy King
Australia's Maverick Millionaire	Margaret Way
Rescued by the Brooding Tycoon	Lucy Gordon
Not-So-Perfect Princess	Melissa McClone
The Heart of a Hero	Barbara Wallace
Swept Off Her Stilettos	Fiona Harper
Mr Right There All Along	Jackie Braun
The Tortured Rebel	Alison Roberts
Dating Dr Delicious	Laura Iding

HISTORICAL

Married to a Stranger	Louise Allen
A Dark and Brooding Gentleman	Margaret McPhee
Seducing Miss Lockwood	Helen Dickson
The Highlander's Return	Marguerite Kaye

MEDICAL™

The Doctor's Reason to Stay	Dianne Drake
Career Girl in the Country	Fiona Lowe
Wedding on the Baby Ward	Lucy Clark
Special Care Baby Miracle	Lucy Clark

AUGUST 2011
LARGE PRINT TITLES

ROMANCE

Jess's Promise	Lynne Graham
Not For Sale	Sandra Marton
After Their Vows	Michelle Reid
A Spanish Awakening	Kim Lawrence
In the Australian Billionaire's Arms	Margaret Way
Abby and the Bachelor Cop	Marion Lennox
Misty and the Single Dad	Marion Lennox
Daycare Mum to Wife	Jennie Adams

HISTORICAL

Miss in a Man's World	Anne Ashley
Captain Corcoran's Hoyden Bride	Annie Burrows
His Counterfeit Condesa	Joanna Fulford
Rebellious Rake, Innocent Governess	Elizabeth Beacon

MEDICAL™

Cedar Bluff's Most Eligible Bachelor	Laura Iding
Doctor: Diamond in the Rough	Lucy Clark
Becoming Dr Bellini's Bride	Joanna Neil
Midwife, Mother...Italian's Wife	Fiona McArthur
St Piran's: Daredevil, Doctor...Dad!	Anne Fraser
Single Dad's Triple Trouble	Fiona Lowe

SEPTEMBER 2011 HARDBACK TITLES

ROMANCE

The Kanellis Scandal	Michelle Reid
Monarch of the Sands	Sharon Kendrick
One Night in the Orient	Robyn Donald
His Poor Little Rich Girl	Melanie Milburne
The Sultan's Choice	Abby Green
The Return of the Stranger	Kate Walker
Girl in the Bedouin Tent	Annie West
Once Touched, Never Forgotten	Natasha Tate
Nice Girls Finish Last	Natalie Anderson
The Italian Next Door...	Anna Cleary
From Daredevil to Devoted Daddy	Barbara McMahon
Little Cowgirl Needs a Mum	Patricia Thayer
To Wed a Rancher	Myrna Mackenzie
Once Upon a Time in Tarrula	Jennie Adams
The Secret Princess	Jessica Hart
Blind Date Rivals	Nina Harrington
Cort Mason – Dr Delectable	Carol Marinelli
Survival Guide to Dating Your Boss	Fiona McArthur

HISTORICAL

The Lady Gambles	Carole Mortimer
Lady Rosabella's Ruse	Ann Lethbridge
The Viscount's Scandalous Return	Anne Ashley
The Viking's Touch	Joanna Fulford

MEDICAL ROMANCE™

Return of the Maverick	Sue MacKay
It Started with a Pregnancy	Scarlet Wilson
Italian Doctor, No Strings Attached	Kate Hardy
Miracle Times Two	Josie Metcalfe

0811 Gen Std LP

SEPTEMBER 2011
LARGE PRINT TITLES

ROMANCE

HISTORICAL

MEDICAL ROMANCE™